Rum and Razors

*Jessica Fletcher
and Donald Bain*

RUM AND
RAZORS

WHEELER
PUBLISHING, INC.
ROCKLAND, MA

★ AN AMERICAN COMPANY ★

Published in Large Print by arrangement with
The Penguin Group in the United States
and Canada.

PUBLISHERS NOTE
This is a work of fiction. Names, characters, places,
and incidents either are the product of the author's
imagination or are used fictitously, and any
resemblance to actual persons, living or dead,
events, or locales is entirely coincidental.

Wheeler Large Print Book Series.

Set in 16 pt. Plantin.

Library of Congress Cataloging-in-Publication Data

Bain, Donald, 1935–
    Rum and razors / Jessica Fletcher and Donald Bain.
      p. (large print) cm.
    ISBN 1-56895-219-8
    1. Large Type books.   I. Title.
[PS3552.A376R86   1995]
813'.54–dc20   95-17172
                                                          CIP

For Zachary and Alexander

Chapter 1

"GLOTCOYB."

Not another one. It was the fifth envelope I'd received in the past two weeks in which a piece of paper with the letters *G-L-O-T-C-O-Y-B* was enclosed. So amateurish, out of a grade-B movie—letters of varying sizes and fonts cut from magazines and newspapers, and pasted next to each other on a sheet of green construction paper. No return address. No signature. Each mailed from a different neighboring town. Obviously the work of an immature prankster with nothing better to do. Get a life, as they say.

Still, my palms felt clammy as I retrieved the dirty white envelope from the mailbox, knowing that yet another nonsensical message was contained in it. The air was damp and chilled; I felt a cough brewing deep in my lungs. It had been a cold winter in Maine, an oxymoron if there ever was one.

I scurried back into the warmth of the house where the fireplace and Vermont Castings woodstove blazed, wrapped my arms about myself and went to refill my teacup. I sat at the kitchen table, the latest of the unexplained envelopes in front of me. I breathed in the rich fragrance of Orange Pekoe drifting up from my cup. What punctuation would the sender of the message use this day? That was what was most upsetting about the mailings, the use of different punctuation each time. The first hadn't used any. The second was "GLOTCOYB" followed by a question mark. A comma followed the third "GLOTCOYB." The fourth letter punctuated the gobbledygook message with a period. Here was the fifth.

I opened it. "GLOTCOYB!!!" The three exclamation points delivered a sense of finality. There was something ominous about it. On the other hand, I reasoned—as we are prone to do when wishing to dismiss unpleasant thoughts—it might mean the end of the letters.

I placed the fifth piece of green paper in a file folder along with the previous four and took it, and my tea to the office where the manuscript of my latest book was neatly stacked next to the manual typewriter I've used to write all my murder mysteries. I sat and stared at the half-finished page in the typewriter. This latest book was close to completion. A solid day's work would wrap it up. It was due tomorrow at my New York publisher. Ordinarily, I would have completed it well in advance of my deadline. But this winter had been anything but ordinary for me.

I'd been progressing nicely with the book when the cough started. Then came the fever. "You've got yourself a good case 'a pneumonia," my good friend and physician, Seth Hazlitt, told me after a thorough examination.

"I can't have pneumonia," I protested. "I'm in the middle of a book." Each word was separated by a cough.

"Ayuh, I'm well aware of that, Jessica. But you're about to put that book aside, climb into bed, take your medicine, and get better."

I started to protest again but was silenced with, "Maybe I better check you into the hospital. Hire guards 'round-the-clock to make sure this stubborn woman does what the doctor orders."

And so I took to my bed, consumed all the antibiotics Seth prescribed, and "got better." It seemed as though I was out of commission for months, although it wasn't that long. To be truthful, I cheated after a week, forcing myself to sit at the typewriter to grind out a painful page or two before succumbing to damnable fatigue and crawling back into bed, happy to be there.

Seth eventually gave me a clean bill of health, along with the admonition that I ease back into my usual busy lifestyle. No longer a prisoner trapped within my own body, I got back to work in earnest on the book, an occasional coughing fit triggered by cold air the only reminder of the compelling endurance test I'd been through. I dove back into the novel, my fingers trying to keep up with my mind as I crafted the final, climactic scene in which my detective-heroine unravels the mystery and, through her dogged pursuit of the truth, points the finger of guilt at the murderer.

Tomorrow's deadline loomed large, of course. But there was another inducement for me to finish. In two days I would be on a plane headed for the Caribbean island of St. Thomas for two weeks of relaxation, rum fruit punch, and spicy West Indian food, balmy ocean breezes, tropical nights on the beach, and a few good books by other writers to read while rocking lazily in a hammock strung between palm trees.

I couldn't wait. Just what the doctor ordered. In fact, Seth had suggested I spend some time in a warm climate. So had my good friends, Walter and Laurie Marschalk, who'd left Cabot Cove three years ago to buy and manage Lover's Lagoon Inn, a small, chic and wildly expensive hotel on St. Thomas.

They had been inviting me to be their guest ever since taking over the inn, but I never seemed to have the time. But after this winter, their salesmanship was no longer needed. I would make the time.

The notion of basking in a balmy clime was, of course, appealing. And so was the contemplation of seeing Walter and Laurie again. Before becoming an innkeeper, Walter had been a highly respected travel writer, his articles appearing in hundreds of publications. His guidebooks to exotic, off-the-beaten-track destinations were considered the best of their genre. When the Marschalks lived in Cabot Grove, Walter was away most of the year. Fortunately, Laurie was the sort of self-sufficient woman who always had a dozen projects going at once. She missed Walter, of course. But there was never a hint of unhappiness or envy. Travel, and writing about it, was what Walter did. Just that simple.

Laurie had her own career. A superb chef, she'd studied at the world's finest cooking schools. Her book on New England cooking, published ten years earlier, was considered a classic. When she and Walter left for St. Thomas, she was in the midst of writing another cookbook, this one a virtual encyclopedia of herbal cooking.

But she'd shelved that project, according to a recent letter I'd received from her, because she'd fallen in love with Caribbean cooking and had signed a publishing contract to write a book on that subject. "I admit, I experiment on my guests," she wrote me, "but so far no fatalities. Can't wait to tickle your palate, Jess."

"GLOTCOYB."

I picked up the folder and examined its contents again. What could this be about? Maybe I should be more concerned, even frightened with so many crazies running around these days. Cabot Cove was a peaceful little community, virtually crime free. But there were the requisite "unusual people" who didn't always act quite normal, at least when judged against the town's norms.

I tried to get back to my writing, but "GLOTCOYB" dominated my thoughts. I had to put it to rest if I were to complete the manuscript, get it off to New York by Federal Express, pack for my trip, and do a zillion other things.

I dialed Cabot Cove's sheriff and my good friend, Morton Metzger. It was time to ring someone else in on what was going on. As silly as the whole thing probably was, a little prudence might be in order.

Mort was out of the office according to his deputy. "Just tell him I called," I said. I then tried a friend with the FBI in Bangor, but he was "out of the country."

A sudden thought caused me to smile. This whole "GLOTCOYB" business had probably been brainstormed by somebody who's read too many mystery books, possibly a fledgling mystery writer looking for a break. I pictured my friendly Federal Express driver arriving at my door with a manuscript titled, "GLOTCOYB." The letters were a misguided attempt to capture my attention and whet my appetite. Maybe not so misguided. If that was the scenario behind the mailings, my attention had certainly been captured. Much to my chagrin.

I'd just returned to my manuscript when the phone rang. I picked it up. "Hello?"

"*Glot-coyb.*" It was a female. Or a man with a high voice.

Click.

I knew one thing. If it *was* a writer looking for my help, he—or she—would get a scathing review from this author.

It wasn't until seven that evening that I typed, with a profound sense of relief and pride, THE END. I'd called my publisher in New York, Vaughan Buckley, whose Buckley House had been my publisher for years, to inform him that the manuscript would be a day late. He laughed. "The way most writers work, Jessica, being one day late is like being two months early. Don't worry about it, and have a great vacation. I envy you."

I looked out the kitchen window. It had rained late in the afternoon but had now stopped. Hopefully the skies would clear for my flight. I was nervous enough in planes, but my knuckles turn especially white when I can't see the wingtips.

Time to pack.

I went to a closet in which I stored my summer wardrobe and started the process. I'd gotten packing down to a science after years of touring to promote my books, using a long typewritten list as my guide. For short trips, I found that saying out loud each day that I would be away, and selecting a day and nighttime wardrobe for each was a helpful supplement to my list. A traveling bag of toiletries was always packed and ready to go.

With packing behind me, dinner loomed large. The cupboard was relatively bare; no sense having food sit around for the two weeks I'd be away.

I opened the freezer door and took out one of two low-calorie frozen dinners that remained there. I placed it in the microwave, set the timer, and returned to my office to prepare the package for pickup in the morning by Federal Express. As I sat at my desk filling out the form, a flash of light from outside caught my eye. Strange, I thought, a bolt of lightning in the middle of winter? I went to the window, held my hand above my eyes, and peered through the glass. The front yard was illuminated by dozens of flash-lights. Police? A search party in search of a fugitive? Then I saw it, a long white banner held aloft by a row of people. On the banner were big, bold black letters: GLOTCOYB.

The doorbell rang. I tensed. My hands became fists. I glanced about the office in search of a weapon. I thought of the fireplace tools in the living room. The doorbell sounded again, longer this time, sustained ringing.

I walked quickly to the living room, picked up a fireplace poker and approached the front door, the poker raised. All right, I thought. I don't know who you are, or what you're doing here, but you won't get what you want without a fight.

I drew a deep breath, reached for the doorknob, and turned it. I slowly pulled the door open and was face-to-face with—Dr. Seth Hazlitt, Sheriff Morton Metzger, schoolboy grins on their faces, satisfaction in their eyes. Behind them stood a

7

crowd of other familiar faces, the banner held aloft with one hand, their other hands clutching bottles of champagne or baskets of food.

"GLOTCOYB," they shouted. "Good luck on the completion of your book."

"I don't believe this," I said.

"Put the poker down, Jess," Morton said. "You could kill a fella with that thing."

Tears began to collect in my eyes, but I managed to control them. A loose cough formed in my chest as the frigid night air reached my lungs. "Come in," I said, standing back to allow them to enter.

Once everyone was inside, and corks popped on the champagne bottles and food was in the oven, Mort asked, "Well, Jess, what'd you think of all those crazy letters you've been gettin'?" A silly grin was still painted all over his broad face.

Should I admit to him that I'd become fearful, and had even called the FBI?

"To tell you the truth, Mort, I really didn't give them much thought. I knew they were the work of some silly prankster—or pranksters. A lot of good it would have done me to be concerned and call *you*." Everyone laughed.

Clam pies, pork and beans, a hearty meat stew, and bowls of fresh salads miraculously appeared on my dining room table. They'd even brought plastic plates and utensils, and plastic glasses for the champagne. "To your good health, safe, pleasant trip and to the completion of another best-seller," Seth said, raising his glass. "Glotcoy*P*!"

"Glotcoy*P*?" I said. "You mean glotcoy*B*, don't you?"

"No, I mean Glotcoy*P*," he said, enunciating

8

the *P.* "Good luck on the completion of your pneumonia."

"*That* I'll drink to," I said, sipping my bubbly.

"Here, here," the crowd chanted, joining me in the toast.

Someone had brought a tape of Calypso music to get me in the mood for my trip, and the party soon became a festive gathering of dear friends who I knew had meant well with their Glotcoyb game. I still harbored a certain anger at having been put through the series of mysterious mailings, but I didn't express it. It was not the time, nor the place. But when I returned from my vacation, I would bring it up with Seth and Morton. It might have truly frightened another person.

As the party wound down, Jed Richardson, a former Pan Am pilot who now owned and operated his own small airline out of Cabot Cove, took me aside. "Sure you don't want me to fly you down to Bangor to catch your plane to St. Thomas?" he asked.

"Not this time, Jed," I said. "Seth really wants to drive me. Besides, he has some shopping to do in Bangor." I didn't add that I would feel more secure in a car. Not that Jed wasn't an excellent pilot. I'd flown often with him, and he had my complete trust despite a few harrowing experiences that had nothing to do with his piloting skill. It was just that considering everything I'd been through this winter, I wasn't up for a cold, bumpy ride in a small, single-engine plane no matter who piloted it.

My guests cleaned up and started to leave. Lots of kisses on the cheek and hugs. "Have a ball in St. Thomas," I was told. "Don't get sunburned," another person told me. "That island sun can gettcha." And, "Not too much demon rum, Jess. It sneaks up on yah."

Seth and Morton were the last to leave. No surprise there. I said to them, "When I return, I expect a welcoming party with another banner."

"Fair enough, Jessica, but what should that banner say?"

"Simply, 'Welcome Home.' But just the banner. No letters. Good night, gentlemen. This lady has a busy day tomorrow. And thanks for being so thoughtful. I'm very fortunate to have friends like you."

Chapter 2

I hadn't been to the Caribbean in many years. Come to think of it, I hadn't taken a vacation anywhere in a long time. My travels always seem to have a business purpose, with an occasional day or two thrown in for rest and sightseeing. Some of my friends from Cabot Cove make a yearly trip to the Caribbean, or to the Bahamas as a respite from the numbing cold of Maine winters. For me, if I'm lucky, there have been occasional business trips to California or Arizona to warm these bones when the snow falls and the winds howl back home.

But here I was heading for a sunny Caribbean isle for no other purpose than to relax, no manuscript to edit, no twisted plot point to unravel, no talk show on which to sell my wares—nothing except personal pleasure.

It made me nervous.

"Ladies and gentlemen, this is the captain. We should be touching down in St. Thomas in about twenty minutes. Hope you've enjoyed flying with us today and that we'll see you again soon."

I looked out my window. The sky was cobalt blue. Thin white gauzy clouds floated above. Below, the water was a medley of blue and green, the sun playing off what looked like millions of emeralds. The plane's dark shadow on the water was an alien intruder.

The captain banked the aircraft hard-left, giving me the proverbial bird's-eye view of the island that would be home for the next two weeks. It seemed to float in the azure sea. It was so perfect it didn't look real, the contrasting colors of verdant green foliage, pastel houses with vivid red roofs, salt-white beaches and aquamarine sea as unnatural as colored contact lenses displayed in optometry shops. The visual splendor of it made me wonder if someone—some *one*—had drafted a blueprint of the most beautiful spot on earth and decided to build it directly below me. Maybe that was how it happened. I never argue those things.

As we maneuvered into our final approach, the reflection off countless pockets of water and beaches dazzled the eye. The beaches seemed deserted; I saw only an occasional person or two wading in the water, or strolling the sand. If privacy was high on anyone's priority list, this was the place. At least it appeared that way from the air.

Then, suddenly, St. Thomas's mountains loomed large and menacing as we made our final approach to Cyril E. King International Airport. The runway appeared to me to be hopelessly short and narrow for the plane. We continued our rapid descent, rugged hills on each side threatening to encapsulate us. I gripped my armrests and braced, closed my eyes and took a deep breath. The wheels momentarily touched the concrete strip, bounced off it, then hugged it for good as the captain reversed the engines to help stop the aircraft before running out of runway. Applause exploded from the other passengers, and there were whoops of glee. I joined in. I was as glad as anyone to again be on terra firma.

The airport did not mirror the idyllic, deserted picture of St. Thomas I had gotten from the air. Although there was a discernible laissez-faire in the way people moved and interacted, there was a corresponding, yet subtle sense of urgency and quiet efficiency. A spirited steel drum band sent bubbling melodies through the terminal as we were briskly herded toward Customs where uniformed men and women prepared to process us. I'd just gotten in line when I heard, "Jess. Jessica. Over here."

Laurie Marschalk waved to me from behind a metal barrier. "Hello," I said loudly. She pointed to the luggage area. "Meet you there."

"The purpose of your visit?" I was asked by a smiling, plump native woman in uniform. She spoke English, of course; St. Thomas is part of the U.S. Virgin Islands. But there was a delightful lilt to her voice, Creole, or West Indian.

I started to say "business" but stopped myself. I returned her smile. "Vacation," I said, surprised at how foreign the word sounded coming from my mouth. "Just a vacation."

She stamped my passport. A valid driver's license would have sufficed, but I don't drive. I passed through her position and soon joined Laurie where baggage from our flight was being unloaded. We hugged, stepped back to observe each other, and hugged again.

"Welcome to St. Thomas," she said.

"Happy to be here. It's like a picture postcard from the air."

"Even nicer close up. See your bags?"

I did, and an eager young man carried them for me to where Laurie had parked her fire engine-red Range Rover beneath a "NO PARKING" sign. A ramrod-straight policeman saw us approach and slowly shook his head. Laurie smiled sweetly. "I didn't see the sign," she said.

"Don't be conning me, Mrs. Marschalk," said the officer.

"Would I lie to you?" she replied. "How's your wife?"

"Just fine. And don't be parking where you shouldn't be."

"I promise," Laurie said, opening the tailgate to allow the porter to load my bags. I looked up into the midday sun and remembered Seth's warnings about not suffering sunburn. My fair skin and the sun have never been friends. I'm meticulous about using sunscreens and covering up. A rivulet of perspiration ran from my forehead into my eyes. "Wheh!" I said. "It's hot."

"Standing here is," Laurie replied. "Come on. It's a lot cooler at the inn. We're up high on the north coast. Always a breeze."

"That policeman seemed to know you pretty well," I said as Laurie navigated traffic and aimed for the airport exit.

"I'm notorious," she said. "Well, at least the car is. Hard to miss."

"Yes. You really didn't have to pick me up. You must be busy running the inn."

"An understatement."

"I could have taken a taxi."

She guffawed. "All the cabdrivers delight in taking tourists on a tour. Doesn't matter what your destination, you get a tour. We wouldn't have seen you for hours."

The move to St. Thomas from Maine had obviously been palatable for Laurie. She never looked better. She'd always enjoyed the natural look.

Her tan was moderate, her gray, shoulder-length hair, pulled back into a tight chignon, was neither permed, moussed, or teased. A tan Banana Republic skirt and shirt, and leather sandals complemented her free-and-easy style, as well as her lithe figure. She was one of those people with a hypermetabolism who burned off everything she ate. I judged her to be about sixty, although it was hard to tell. She looked younger than when I'd last seen her in Maine three years ago. Perhaps having been a model in her youth helped. Or maybe living on a tropical island arrests the aging process.

We followed a road that took us in an easterly direction from the airport. At first, I thought Laurie wasn't paying attention to her driving. We were on the left side of the road, the wrong side. But Laurie sat in the left seat. The steering wheel was where it ought to be, at least back home. She read my thoughts, laughed, and said, "You get used to it."

The route was along the coast—The Caribbean Sea that separated St. Thomas from St. Croix to the south was on our right. We passed through the small town of Altona, whose narrow streets sloped gently down to Crown Bay, and then reached Frenchtown with its pretty pastel houses, most boasting some form of black wrought-iron decoration.

We arrived at the capital of the U.S. Virgin Islands, Charlotte Amalie, a bustling, picturesque small city crowded with tourists who poured off two huge cruise ships docked in the harbor. The streets were chockablock with shops and small restaurants. Dozens of street vendors dominated the dock. Cobblestone alleys with hundreds of hanging green plants linked the main shopping streets. There were signs offering every type of merchandise—cameras, clothing, electronic equipment, and jewelry. Jewelry stores every-where. Small wonder St. Thomas was famous as a duty-free shopping mecca.

Not that that aspect of the trip appealed to me. My favorite shopping sprees involve going through catalogues from L.L. Bean, Land's End, J. Crew, and Orvis in search of clothing to suit my style. I've been on the mailing list for Victoria's Secret for years and keep meaning to write to suggest I don't meet its demographic profile.

"Get some shopping in, Jess," Laurie said, reading my thoughts.

"I might just do that," I said.

After passing Government Hill and heading north on Mafolie Road, the scenery began to change. The vegetation became more lush, and the hills played a more dominant role in the land-scape. And it was cooler. Laurie had used the Range Rover's air-conditioning until reaching this point. Now, she turned it off and opened the windows. "Smell that, Jess," she said, drawing in a long, sustained breath. I did as instructed. The air was sweet with the floral scent of red hibiscus, purple bougainvillea, and fragrant fran-gipani. It smelled and tasted fresh, and was cooler and less oppressive than at the airport or in the city.

As the trip progressed, Laurie fell silent. I observed her as she concentrated on driving—a prudent thing to do on the island's winding roads—and noticed deep worry lines in her fore-head. Nothing unusual about that, of course.

Aging will add wrinkles no matter how little worrying we do. But there was an expression on her pretty face that spoke of concern about things other than avoiding cars that careened around curves as though they weren't there. I felt compelled to initiate conversation. "Remember the last time we saw each other?" I asked.

"Of course I do," she said. "What a snowstorm." Two days before Laurie and Walt were to move from Cabot Cove to St. Thomas, I had invited them to my house for a traditional clambake, as traditional as it could be considering the time of year, and that it would have to be held indoors rather than on a beach.

We had such a good time that we never bothered to check the progress of a storm that had begun dumping snow in the morning. Not to worry. Walter and Laurie lived only a few miles from me. Besides, us Down-easters are used to snow. Doesn't faze us.

But this storm did. The snow had fallen at a rate of three inches an hour. By the time my guests were ready to leave, the roads were impassable. Walt wanted to walk home, but Laurie and I dissuaded him (even though he'd consumed enough alcohol to get him through a night in a snowdrift.) They stayed overnight. The next morning, Walt got up early to dig out their car, fell, broke three ribs, and suffered a mild concussion.

"Bet you don't miss the foul weather," I said.

Her reply was a shake of the head. The lines in her forehead deepened, and I discerned a tremble of her lip.

Should I ask? When in doubt, I always do.

"Laurie, is everything all right? I mean, you seem disturbed about something."

It was a rueful laugh. "Is it obvious? I'd hoped it wouldn't be."

"Enough to prompt me to ask."

She said nothing.

"I would certainly understand," I said, "if this was not a good time for me to be visiting you and Walter. I could stay somewhere else. We could get together when it's convenient for you."

We stopped to allow a farmer to cross his goats. Laurie turned and looked at me. Her eyes were moist. I'd been right. She was on the verge of tears. "I'm sorry," she said. "I—we've been under a lot of pressure lately, Jess. I know I'm not myself. Nothing to do with you or your visit. And I don't want to hear another word about staying someplace else. We've been looking forward to having you visit us ever since we moved here. In some ways, you might be just what the doctor ordered."

"Sure?" I asked. "If you and Walter need some time alone to work things out, I would—"

The goats passed safely, and a driver behind beeped his horn. Laurie accelerated. "We're not under *that* kind of pressure," she said. "The marriage is safe. It's the business that's not."

I nodded. "It's such a difficult economic time," I said. "So many people experiencing trouble these days." I wasn't sure how deep to delve into it. "I imagine the travel business is one of the first to suffer the repercussions of a recession," I offered. "Travel isn't something people need when they're concerned about a roof over their head and putting food on the table."

"You're very right, Jess. But even people with

18

money, and a roof over their heads, are scaling back on their travels. Lover's Lagoon is no place for bargain hunters. We get—or at least we ask top dollar."

"I'm sure it's worth every penny," I said. "I'm surprised you have a room for me. It's the height of the season, isn't it?"

"Right again, but our bookings are down. More than one vacancy I can assure you." We drove in silence for another minute before she said, "Frankly, the problems we're having aren't just financial, although that's part of it. Doing business in the Caribbean can be tricky. Lots of political intrigue, even outright corruption."

I laughed. "Not unique for St. Thomas," I said. I mentioned a politician we both knew in Cabot Cove who was caught siphoning parking violation fees into his pocket.

"If only it was as simple as that," she said, her tone suggesting this topic of conversation was over.

After another fifteen minutes, Laurie pulled into a winding driveway lined with trees and plants, the likes of which I'd never seen. I asked about them. The Laurie I knew from Cabot Cove, who was as avid a gardener as she was a cook, would have stopped and given a detailed explanation of each piece of vegetation. Instead, obviously anxious to get back to her duties as the inn's mistress, she said quickly, "The ones with the scarlet flowers and drooping pods are flamboyants. Those others are manzanillos. They're poisonous."

Before I had a chance to comment, she said, "I have to run." She gave me a fast hug. An elderly black man with white hair and wearing a red jacket, white shirt, black tie, and black slacks came from the main entrance. "This is Thomas," Laurie said. "He'll take your bags and get you settled. We've given you cottage ten, the last villa on your right." She pointed to a pink house at the end of a row of them that looked as though it could accommodate a family of eight. "Settle in, unwind, relax. Dinner's at eight-thirty. Bye."

While Thomas placed my hang-up clothing in a large closet and tended to other things, I examined my villa. It would have been nice to have someone with whom to share it, I thought. It was spacious and welcoming, a lovely, calm oasis. The master bedroom was stark white, which rendered the room's appointments—pale blue porcelain lamps, a darker blue throw that had been purposefully placed over one of two white wicker chairs, and bold, modern paintings that I judged to be Haitian—that much more visible and attractive. The floor was a cool white-and-blue terra-cotta. Fluffy throw rugs were at the foot and side of a king-size pencil-post bed canopied with wispy white fabric. Thomas had switched on a large ceiling fan that spun lazily above me. But I noticed an air-conditioning switch. Just in case the fan didn't do the trick.

There were two smaller bedrooms decorated in the same hues as the master.

The living room was larger than mine in Cabot Cove. It, too, was white, but the accents were bloodred, including vases overflowing with crimson flowers. Another ceiling fan directed a gentle breeze down on me. A large red lacquered desk dominated one corner. "My own fax machine?" I said.

"Yes, ma'am," Thomas replied, smiling. "And

your own VCR in the bedroom and this room. Movies are in the main house. Take those you wish to watch."

"It's lovely."

"Yes, ma'am, it is. Would you care for a cocktail?"

"That sounds wonderful."

"Your preference?"

"Make it *your* preference. Something distinctly St. Thomas."

He grinned. "I'll be right back."

I used his absence to examine the bath. It, like the other rooms, was oversized. The shower stall, with jets coming at you from all sides as well as from above, would accommodate a party. A separate magenta marble tub was spacious and sunken, and doubled as a spa and whirlpool. Smaller vases of island flowers added splashes of color against white wall tiles. A vanity tucked away in the corner had a skirt flowing from it. The pattern, petite, pastel pink rosebuds on an even paler pink background, would have made a nice addition to my vacation wardrobe.

Thomas returned with a tall glass filled with a frothy, lemony liquid, and adorned with fruit. "Looks yummy," I said.

"It is, ma'am. It's called a Lover's Lagoon. Dark and light rums, coconut milk, pineapple, kahlua, and a few other ingredients. It was created here at the inn and won the Caribbean competition held each year."

"A competition for new drinks?"

"Yes, ma'am. Is there anything else I can get you?"

"I think not, but thank you. You've been very gracious."

"Enjoy your afternoon, Mrs. Fletcher." He backed out of the villa.

Was Thomas his real name, I wondered? If I'd been on St. John, a short ferry ride to the east of St. Thomas, would his name have been John? Thomas had opened French doors in the bedroom. I stepped out onto a large terrace. It had three walls which made it into a room of sorts. The fourth "wall" was the breathtaking view.

The floors were bleached wood. A glass table and four chairs, as well as several wicker lounge chairs with cushions covered in the same fabric as the rosebud skirt in the bathroom, were inviting. A dozen hanging pots held riots of color, purple and yellow, blue and red.

I went to the open end of the terrace and involuntarily gasped at the view. Immediately in front of me was a small, gently curved lagoon that might have been painted by an artist from the Impressionist school. Lover's Lagoon, from which the inn took its name? Undoubtedly. Blue-green water gently lapped on to a chalk white strip of sand no more than twenty feet deep. Trees with large, glossy leathery leaves, and purple fruit that hung in grape-like bunches, ringed the lagoon with perfect symmetry. They were aptly called sea grape trees, I would learn.

No wonder Laurie often referred to the lagoon in her letters. She'd indicated in one of them that there was a native superstition attached to the lagoon. Something about standing in its waters and kissing ensuring a long, loving life together. A nice thought. How fortunate for Walter and Laurie to have been able to purchase such a prime piece of land on which to build the inn of their dreams.

I changed into a multicolored Indonesian batik wrap provided guests by the inn, took my Lover's Lagoon cocktail and a book I'd been reading on the flight to one of the chaise lounge chairs and settled in, enjoying the sensation of all the tensions of the past year draining from my body.

When I awoke, the drink missing only one sip and my book unopened, the sun had fallen into the lagoon, splashing its water and sand with crimson. I started to laugh, held my drink in a toast to the serene setting before me, and said aloud, "To life."

Chapter 3

When I arrived at the inn's small dining room, Walter was seated alone at a table. I assumed Laurie was in the kitchen. He stood and extended his arms. "Hello, Jessica!" he said. "A sight for sore eyes." We embraced. He then took my hand and kissed it. Moving to St. Thomas hadn't altered that aspect of Walter Marschalk. He was known as Cabot Cove's resident hand-kisser, sometimes to the chagrin of certain Cabot Cove ladies.

"Come, sit," he said, holding out a chair that afforded a splendid view of Lover's Lagoon and the Atlantic Ocean beyond.

"Beauty in every direction," I said. "I had no idea you'd ended up with such a magnificent property, Walter. You must wake up every morning and marvel at it."

"Depends on how many bills arrived the previous day," he said. His inflection was light-hearted, but I sensed he'd forced it. Maybe it was his physical appearance that told me so. He looked haggard, a man who'd suffered one too many recent defeats. Walter had always been a strong, solidly built man, but he'd lost weight. Too much weight. His hair had changed, too. It had been coal-black—I was certain he hadn't dyed it back in Cabot Cove because men who dye their hair are always so easy to spot. At least for me they are. His hair was now almost completely gray and in need of a trim. That was probably the most telltale sign of all that something was wrong. This man who'd prided himself on a fastidious appearance was now unkempt. Caribbean-casual? Tropical laid-back? Somehow, I didn't think so.

But the twinkle in his hazel eyes hadn't disappeared. Walter had always had mischievous eyes. It was good to see the sparkle still there.

"Settled in?" he asked.

"Very much so. The room—the *rooms* are lovely. I fell asleep on the terrace."

"That's what terraces are for. Excuse me." He got up to seat a man and woman who'd arrived for dinner.

"Is Laurie in the kitchen?" I asked when he returned.

"No. She's having dinner in town. Business."

"Oh. You must wear a dozen hats every day. Do you do the cooking when she's gone?"

"On occasion. Excuse me." He disappeared through swinging doors into what I assumed was the kitchen, returning with a native waiter dressed in a tuxedo. Anger was etched on Walter's face when he again rejoined me.

"Please don't feel obligated to entertain me, Walter. Just go about your business, and I'll—"

"I don't know how many times I have to remind the help that the guests come first," he said.

"Is finding good help a problem?" I asked.

"One of many, Jess." He motioned the waiter to the table. "This is Mrs. Fletcher," he said. "She's a special guest and will share our table each night she's here."

"A pleasure, Mrs. Fletcher," the waiter said, his bright smile made more so because of the contrast between white teeth and black skin. "Welcome to Lover's Lagoon. Would you care for a cocktail before dinner?"

"Wine with dinner," I said. "White."

Walter selected a white zinfandel, and the waiter left the table.

"Laurie hinted at how difficult it is running an inn," I said.

"She did?"

"Well, she didn't go into any detail. Just—hinted." A man had arrived for dinner and stood at the doorway. Walter didn't seem to notice, so I said, "You have a guest."

Walter replied gruffly, "He knows where he sits."

The man glared at Walter as he crossed the dining room and sat at a table on the opposite side of the room. I thought of Walter's earlier comment about guests always being first priority and wondered at this surprising breach of that creed. Walter knew what I was thinking. "He's a spy," he said matter-of-factly.

"A spy? For whom?"

"Diamond Reef. The monstrosity next door."

"It's huge," I said. "At least what I saw of it from my terrace."

"Huge, and arrogant. We've been at war ever since I bought Lover's Lagoon. They wanted this property."

"And that gentleman is here spying for them?"

"I'm pretty sure he is."

I observed the man, who was giving the waiter his drink order. He didn't look like a spy to me, although I admit to not having known many. Spies, that is. Was this a case of Walter's overactive imagination? Middle-age paranoia?

"Diamond Reef is run by a bunch of charlatans," he said.

Our wine arrived, snuggled in shaved ice in a silver bucket. The evening's special appetizer was served. A small, handwritten menu indicated it was a conch fritter adorned with ancho chile mayonnaise, cilantro pesto, and fresh lime.

"I've never tasted conch before," I said.

"It's pronounced conk," Walter said. "It's really quite good the way Laurie prepares it." He was right. It was delicious.

"You were telling me about the owners of the resort next door," I said after tasting and enthusiastically endorsing Walter's choice of wine. Walter had seated other guests and now seemed ready to relax, at least for more than a few minutes.

"Right," he said. "They're out to take Lover's Lagoon from me."

"That beautiful body of water?"

"Not just the lagoon, Jess. Our inn. They've resorted to all sorts of tactics to kill our business. They just finished building villa-type units adjacent to their main building. I sent a friend to stay in one of them. He told me they've copied our units right down to the lamps and towels." Obviously, spying on competitors wasn't alien to Walter. Maybe he was right about the man across the room.

"Do you really pose that much of a threat to Diamond Reef?" I asked. "I mean, this is a small inn. How much business could you realistically take away from them?"

"It isn't taking business from them that has them up in arms. It's the lagoon itself." He leaned closer and used a conspiratorial tone. "Between you and me, Jess, it took some heavy string pulling to get this property. Until we bought it, it was held in an environmental trust by the U.S. Virgin's legislature. On top of that, the lagoon was covered by a conservation decree, sort of a national landmark. It's the prettiest lagoon in the Caribbean, in the world as far as I'm concerned. Add to that all the island myths about its mystical powers to grant a long and loving life, and you have prime property."

"And?"

"And how did we manage to get it?"

I nodded.

"Well, I've had a friend for many years in the Virgin Island Senate. His name is Bobby Jensen. In fact, Laurie and I have become close with both Bobby and his wife, Pamela. At any rate, guests at Diamond Reef always had direct access to the lagoon. Management there used the lagoon's legend to help market the resort. They didn't own it, but no one raised an eyebrow when their guests went down to take a swim. Then we came along. With Bobby Jensen's help, the legislature lifted the decree and took the lagoon and this adjacent property out of the environmental trust. We knew it was about to happen and had the inside track. The minute the property was free of government entanglements, we bought it."

"Quite a coup," I said.

"Sure was. But you can imagine how our friends next door reacted. They screamed bloody murder, threatened all kinds of actions including bodily harm. Now that we sit between them and the lagoon, their guests no longer have access to it."

I silently wondered why Walter didn't simply

28

work out an arrangement with Diamond Reef to grant their guests access to the lagoon. "Owning" water has never seemed fair to me. But I said nothing. The two resorts were obviously locked in an intense competitive struggle. Business. It's a good thing I'm a writer. I would have been an abject failure as a businesswoman.

Walter seated more guests, and tended to business in the kitchen. I perused that evening's menu specialties in his absence. There was callaloo soup (Laurie noted on the menu that callaloo was similar to spinach), boneless breast of chicken blackened with Creole spices and accompanied by black beans and avocado salsa, a Caesar salad, and for dessert coconut flan. A second printed menu offered less adventurous standard fare.

Over soup, I asked Walter whether he was in danger of losing the property.

"Sure," he replied. "Diamond Reef's management and attorneys are determined to have our purchase declared illegal. They're trying to turn it into a national scandal, a Virgin Islands' Watergate. They're pulling out all the stops. Just yesterday they sent out a press release accusing Bobby of graft and corruption, and branding Laurie and me as interlopers who paid bribes to acquire Lover's Lagoon."

"You could sue for libel," I suggested.

"We don't have enough money to sue anyone, Jess. Things are tight. There have been some— well, I don't mind sharing this with you. There have been incidents over the past year that have turned some of our guests sour on the inn. Dead animals and birds found floating in the lagoon, an oil slick mysteriously appearing, even a few confrontations between our guests and unknown native assailants. Doesn't take many things like that to make sure those guests don't return. And word gets around fast. Every time something happens, it makes the papers and all the travel publications. It's been hell."

"You think Diamond Reef is behind those incidents?"

"Absolutely. I can't prove it yet, but I'm getting close."

"I feel terrible for you and Laurie."

"*We* feel terrible for us. You know me pretty well, Jess. I've always been just a small-town boy from Cabot Cove, Maine. Can you picture me, or Laurie, bribing government officials?" His laugh rendered the question ludicrous.

"Of course not," I said, not necessarily because I found the notion as ridiculous as he did. Walter and Laurie Marschalk have always been two of my favorite people. I'd always found them to be scrupulously honest and fair. But I also recognized that Walter was not without ambition, especially when it came to Lover's Lagoon.

I remembered him returning to Cabot Cove from his frequent travels and talking incessantly about the tiny jewel he'd discovered on St. Thomas, and his determination to one day build an inn on it. It was an obsession.

I'd never seen them so ebullient as the day the deal went through and they announced to their friends in Cabot Cove that Lover's Lagoon was theirs, and that they were preparing to leave Maine.

It occurred to many of us that such an ambitious undertaking would require vast sums of money. Not that the Marschalks were without it. Walter and Laurie always enjoyed the good life, and seemed to have the resources to support it. Their home in Cabot Cove had six bedrooms, four fireplaces, and was situated on thirty acres on the highest point in town, offering them magnificent views of the harbor, and mountains in the distance. I'd asked about the cost of purchasing the property and building a luxurious inn on it.

"Outside investors," Walter had replied, and that was the end of that conversation.

Walter surveyed the dining room before continuing with his saga of troubles at Lover's Lagoon. "Things have gotten so out of hand that I received this in my mail today." He handed me a yellow post-it note. "YOU'RE A DEAD MAN MARSCHALK," was written in black ink in small, careful handwriting.

Walt leaned over and asked, "Think it's legit, Jessica? Should I take it seriously? You know about these things."

"I'd take any death threat seriously, Walter. Especially considering the circumstances."

He scowled. "I know you're right, Jess, but I'll be damned if I'll let—" He stopped as a pair of hands belonging to a tall, slim man rested on his shoulders. I judged this visitor to our table to be about forty. His deep, bronze tan might have been painted on his angular face. Coal-black hair was streaked with the perfect amount of gray at the temples to add a requisite touch of wisdom to his chronological age. His clothing was studied casual; pleated chinos, blue-and-white shirt opened enough to reveal an acceptable number of chest hairs. His jacket was blue silk. He'd rolled its cuffs up over the cuffs of his shirt, providing a colorful flourish at his wrists.

"How did I know I'd find you here on a beautiful night, with a beautiful woman," the stranger said. He directed his words, and his smile at me.

"Hello, Chris." Walter sounded as enthusiastic as a toll collector in summer at a busy bridge.

The stranger, whose name I now knew was Chris, and who carried a manila envelope, pulled out one of two remaining wrought-iron chairs and sat. "Chris Webb," he said, extending his hand, which I took. "I'm Walter's partner in Lover's Lagoon." Before I could respond, he said, "And you, of course, are the famous and talented Jessica Fletcher." He opened the envelope he'd brought to the table. "When I learned you would be our guest, I ran out and bought a copy of your latest book."

"Good," I said.

"This may be a Caribbean island, but we do have bookstores," he said, his smile ever-present. "I'm not much of a reader—no time—but I'd love you to autograph it. I've collected a few autographs over the years."

I returned his smile, accepted the book and pen he handed me, and wrote: "For Chris Webb. Best wishes, Jessica Fletcher."

"That's great," he said, returning the book to the envelope. Somehow, I wouldn't have been surprised if he went right out and sold the book at a premium autographed price. He had that look about him. Too slick and oily for this lady. I looked at Walter, who rolled his eyes and shook his head.

Webb abruptly turned from me and directed his attention to Walter. I sat back, sipped my wine, and listened to their conversation.

"Walter, my man, glad to see the place is still

standing," said Webb, patting Walter on the back. He might have been young, but he certainly had the old-boy network mannerisms down pat.

"When did you get in?" Walter asked in a voice that said he really didn't care.

"A couple of hours ago." To me: "I live in Miami, Mrs. Fletcher."

"Please call me Jessica." But not Jess, I thought. That's reserved for friends.

"And I'm Chris."

I nodded. I'd hoped he'd again direct his conversation to Walter, but it wasn't to be. "I'm half responsible for this mess called Lover's Lagoon," he told me, laughing and examining nails that had been buffed to a high gloss. "I'm sure Walter's bored you to tears with his tales of travail and woe." He seemed a lot less concerned about the "travail and woe" than Walter.

"To the contrary," I said. "All I know is that if you're Walter's partner, you're partners in a wonderful place. I feel very fortunate to be here."

"We're glad to have you, Jessica. You dress up the place." I expected him to kiss my hand, but he didn't.

The waiter arrived with a place setting for Webb, but he waved him away. "I won't be staying," he said. "I have a dinner engagement in Charlotte Amalie. I just wanted to come by and see how my buddy and partner, Walter, was making out, and to personally welcome this famous lady to Lover's Lagoon."

"Believe it or not, Jess, Chris is the *silent* partner in this endeavor," Walter said. We all laughed. It was nice to see Walter unwind a little. His mood to this juncture had been unrelieved somber. Maybe it was the wine. No matter. I was beginning to feel uncomfortable.

"On second thought, I'd love a martini before I go," Chris announced. "Mind if I linger?"

"Not at all," I said. Walter summoned the waiter with a wave of his hand.

At first, the conversation was pleasant. Chris Webb toasted me and my books. I toasted Lover's Lagoon and wished it, and its owners, eternal life and happiness. There was lighthearted banter. Walter told a joke I didn't think was especially funny, but laughed anyway.

And then the tenor of the table quickly turned. It happened when Walter questioned the competence of the public relations agency in Miami that handled the Lover's Lagoon account.

"Just leave marketing to me," Webb said. It was the first time he hadn't smiled since arriving at the table.

"Nothing's happening," Walter said. "They're ripping us off, giving us nothing for our money."

"Are you saying that I'm ripping you off?" Webb asked.

"You picked 'em," Walter replied. "You pay 'em. With *our* money."

"I resent this," said Webb, downing the remains of his drink.

"I don't give a damn what you resent," said Walter.

It went downhill from there. The atmosphere at the table had thickened to storm-cloud consistency, like the clouds that now hung precariously low over the lagoon. The daily afternoon rainstorm that normally cooled things off in the islands was behind schedule this day. But not at our table.

The conversation continued to heat up. Harsh words were exchanged between the two men as though I wasn't there. A side of Walter emerged that I'd never seen before. He used profanities without regard for my female presence.

My discomfort level was reaching its stretching point.

Then, Walter slammed his fist on the table and said far too loudly for the romantic, peaceful setting of the dining room, "Excuse us, Jess. I'll be back." Other diners joined me as we watched the two partners brusquely stand, leave the table, exit through French doors to a patio, and walk in the direction of the lagoon. They stopped at the water's edge, then disappeared into darkness.

I was slightly embarrassed sitting there alone, but occupied myself with my dinner. Laurie certainly had a way with food. The myriad dishes placed before me tasted like nothing I'd experienced before. I'd just finished my main course when Walter returned. "Sorry, Jess," he said. "This mess we're in gets the best of me sometimes." He sat and wiped his brow with his cloth napkin. Chris was nowhere in sight.

"Don't be silly," I said. "Please don't worry about me. You've got enough on your mind." So much, in fact, he didn't respond. I wasn't even sure he'd heard me.

Walter escorted me back to my room after dinner. Although there had been no further mention of any business troubles in Walter's life, the tick in his eye and constant shuffling of his feet said much.

As he was about to bestow upon my hand his customary kiss, a tall shadow moved between palm trees that had been planted to disguise unsightly garbage dumpsters and air-conditioning units necessary for the operation of the inn.

"Walter," I whispered. "There's someone behind that tree over there."

He whipped his head around assuming the worst. Then he noticeably relaxed. "That's Jacob," he said. "An employee. He'll be history by tomorrow."

"Oh?"

"A surly young man with a chip on his shoulder. A big attitude. He's a gardener, talked a good story when I hired him. He came across as a decent local kid." Walter guffawed. "Kid? He's got three kids of his own. He started off all right but that attitude of his got in the way. Can't tell him anything. I told him more than once that unless he shaped up, he was gone. He just laughed at me, said that he'd file a grievance with the government's labor department. Not easy for a foreigner to fire a native, Jess. Miles of red tape, hearings, proof of cause for dismissal. The government is always after foreign business owners to provide more benefits to local workers. Next thing I know, they'll want us to provide health insurance, life insurance, even child care."

I didn't express my thought that workers should have such benefits.

"But I've had it with him," Walter said. "I intend to fire him tomorrow, no matter what wrath it incurs with the government. He's set some of the guests on edge, and I can't risk alienating anybody."

Because Jacob seemed to have been hiding behind the trees, I was startled when he stood erect and approached us. "Good evening," he said.

I returned his greeting. Walter said nothing. Jacob sauntered past us in the direction of the main house.

"He seems nice enough," I said, knowing immediately it was an inappropriate comment. I didn't know the young man. Walter did.

"Good night, Jess." He kissed my hand. "Sleep tight your first night in paradise."

"I'm sure I will. Good night, Walter. And thank you. Will I see Laurie tomorrow?"

"Sure. At breakfast."

My room was even more perfect than I had remembered it. Someone had turned down my bed and placed several hibiscus flowers on my pillow, alongside Godiva chocolate. An oversize basket brimming with fresh fruit, and a bottle of the same wine I'd enjoyed at dinner had been delivered. Fresh orange and purple hibiscus had been artfully arranged in a crystal vase on my night table.

I opened the doors to my terrace and stepped outside. What a shame, I thought, that man was capable of destroying such beauty. Not that Walter had been ecologically irresponsible in creating Lover's Lagoon Inn. It was just that the blatant ill feelings and politics surrounding it tainted its beauty. Like a lover's triangle—two men fighting over the same goddess.

I intended to do exactly what Walter had suggested—sleep tight my first night in paradise. But I was wide-awake, and suspected that the waiter at dinner might not have poured me decaffeinated cappuccino with dessert. I knew that the way my heart was racing, my eyes weren't due to close for at least several hours. Caffeine before bed always makes me a candidate for a pacemaker.

A walk was in order. My digestive system would be forever grateful. I knew I could stroll the property but it wasn't very large, and was so quiet except for the gentle lapping of water on the beach. It was too much like a library for a nocturnal stroll.

And then the familiar beat and lilting melodies of calypso music wafted on to the terrace from the Diamond Reef next door. I smiled, felt like a child responding to the pied piper. If spies were plying their trade between the two properties, it wouldn't hurt for me to do a little spying of my own. Nothing wrong with that—not when you needed a walk, and with the music so inviting.

I have always been good at rationalizing my actions.

Chapter 4

Diamond Reef was as different from Lover's Lagoon Inn as New York City is from Cabot Cove. It was huge. The main hotel rose above the palms (didn't they have laws prohibiting the height of buildings exceeding the trees?) The new villas Walter had mentioned stretched in a lazy curve from the main building down to a long, pretty beach.

It was on the expansive terrace that the difference between the two properties was most evident. There were people everywhere, most of them young and, I assumed, single. They were a good-looking lot, tanned and fit, the men posturing to display their muscles, the young women sashaying in their bikinis. A mating ritual in full bloom.

Despite the many people mingling about, fruity drinks in hand, the terrace was large enough to not appear crowded. Most people gathered near the bandstand where a native band in colorful costumes played spirited island rhythms. I chose a rattan chair at an empty table on the perimeter of the dance floor. A pretty young woman in short shorts and a halter top, and carrying a tray, suddenly appeared and asked for my order. "Mineral water and lime," I said. I sat back, closed my eyes, and drew a deep breath. A cool, refreshing breeze tickled my face. While I preferred the quiet calm of Walter's inn, this was satisfying, too. Just being away was pleasurable.

The waitress returned with my drink. "Put this on your room?" she asked.

"No, thank you. I'm not staying here." As I reached into my purse, a male voice from behind said, "On the house, Mrs. Fletcher."

I turned to look up at a very tall young man on crutches and wearing a cast on his right foot. He smiled. "You are Jessica Fletcher?" he said.

"Yes."

"Hope I'm not intruding," he said in a deep radio announcer's voice. "I've read all your books and recognized you from the book jackets and television. My name is Mark Dobson. I'm the general manager of Diamond Reef."

"Well, it's a pleasure to meet you," I said. "And thank you for the drink. It wasn't necessary."

"My pleasure. If I'd known you were going to be here, I would have instructed the staff to comp you. You're staying next door, at Marschalk's place."

"That's right. How did you know?"

"Small island, Mrs. Fletcher. Word gets around."

"Like my hometown of Cabot Cove."

"Mind if I sit down?"

"Of course not."

He lowered himself with difficulty into the chair next to me and placed his crutches on the ground. I asked what had happened to him.

"Oh, this?" he replied, raising the foot with the cast. "It comes off next week." He laughed. "The cast, hopefully not the foot. Had a waterskiing accident. My leg got twisted, and I took a bad fall."

He seemed too large a person to be on water

40

skis, but I didn't express my thought. The waitress brought him what I assumed was his usual drink, amaretto over ice. He raised his glass to me. "Welcome to St. Thomas, Mrs. Fletcher, although you might have chosen a better place to stay."

I said, "I'm quite happy staying at Lover's Lagoon. The Marschalks are wonderful hosts—good friends actually—and I'm very impressed with the accommodations, food, and service."

"Just what impresses you, Jessica?" I didn't mind his sudden familiarity, although he was a little quick to put us on a first-name basis.

"Lover's Lagoon is—well, it's simply beautiful. How's that for a writer's descriptive powers?"

"I'm impressed," he said with a gentle laugh. "Actually, it is beautiful. The lagoon, that is. Lover's Lagoon is a cherished spot in this part of the world. I feel bad for the Marschalks."

"Why?"

"I suppose you aren't aware of the problems they've been having. When they first opened up, they did pretty well. But I understand things have gotten bad lately. I hate to see anybody fail."

"And you think they will fail?"

He nodded solemnly. "They bought the land and lagoon under false pretenses. It's all breaking now. You'll hear about it."

I said nothing.

"You said you were personal friends of the Marschalks. I hope I haven't offended you with what I've said."

The fact was he had offended me, and I wanted the conversation to end. "Thank you for the drink," I said. "I really should be getting back."

"Of course. Oh, by the way, I'd be honored to have you as my guest at dinner while you're a guest on the island. There's a large contingent of travel writers staying with us for a conference on the island's future, sponsored by the U.S. Virgin Islands' Office of Tourism."

"I'm sure Walter Marschalk will know many of them," I said. "He was one of the best travel writers in the world before he bought Lover's Lagoon."

"Yes, I know. He stayed at Diamond Reef many times, and wrote a lot about us." I judged from his tone that everything Walter had written about Diamond Reef hadn't been favorable.

"Will you join us, Jessica? We'll be having cocktails each night at seven right here on the patio. Dinner at eight."

"Thank you for the invitation, but I'll be having dinner at Lover's Lagoon tomorrow."

"Well, the invitation is an open one. It doesn't have to involve the travel writers. They'll be with us for five days. I know they'd be delighted to meet you. But if you prefer to stay to yourself, that's fine, too. Just give me a call any night, and you'll have a prime table." He handed me his business card.

"Thank you, Mr. Dobson. Good night."

"One other thing," he said.

"Yes?"

"If you become unhappy where you're staying, you'll always have a room at Diamond Reef." His smile was as smug as his voice. "You wouldn't be the first person to seek asylum with us."

I doubted what he'd said, didn't believe for a moment that guests actually left Lover's Lagoon Inn for Diamond Reef. Maybe the conversation had unduly soured me, but comparing Diamond Reef to Walter and Laurie's inn was like comparing the Bombay Holiday Inn to the Taj Mahal.

I sat on my terrace and contemplated my conversation with Mark Dobson. As much as I wanted to dismiss what he'd said, I couldn't help but wonder whether Walter and Laurie were in far deeper trouble than they'd been willing to admit to me. I hoped not. There was too much trouble in the world for yet another war over territory. I fell asleep to the sound of tree frogs outside my window and the cooling breeze from the ceiling fan. I felt like I'd arrived in Paradise. Or Paradise Lost?

Chapter 5

The shouts came suddenly and grew louder. What in heaven's name? I sat straight up in bed and looked at my small traveling alarm clock. 6:25 A.M.

"I demand a better explanation," said a defiant male voice. "No one has ever complained about me. Tell me who. Name just one person."

"I'm not going to get into it any further, Jacob." This was Walter talking. "I've tried to explain to you as nicely as I can why I'm dismissing you. Now, goddamn it, gather your things and leave my property at once. I'll call the police if you don't."

"You'll be sorry you're doing this, Mr. Marschalk. You'll be sorry's all I can say."

If I hadn't known better, I'd have thought I'd been awakened in New York City where such wake-up calls can be the rule rather than the exception. Why did Walter choose to fire the young man in front of my villa? Surely it wasn't the most convenient place. My villa was the greatest distance from the main inn in which Walter's office was located. Did he choose to do it outside my door for my benefit? If so, the larger question was why? And who else had he awakened? Not an especially thoughtful way to run an inn, I thought.

So much for sleeping late. I hadn't set the alarm because I'd intended to have the birds wake me with a good-morning song.

The angry voices faded as Walter and Jacob departed the area. Finally, there was silence, except for the sweet sounds of the birds serenading me from the terrace. I made a valiant attempt to fall back to sleep but it was obvious that this lady was up for the day. Shades of Cabot Cove and my early to bed, early to rise routine. I was in the process of a final stretch when the phone rang.

"Hello?"

"Jessica, it's Laurie. Hope I didn't wake you."

I was tempted to say, "No, but your husband did." It remained an unstated thought. Instead, I said, "I was just getting up. Bad habits die hard."

"The reason I'm calling so early is to tell you that Walter and I have to go to Miami today to meet with our attorney. A last-minute decision. We're catching a plane this morning and won't be back until tomorrow."

"Anything wrong?" I asked.

"No. In fact, everything is all right now that we've decided to take the bull by the horns and resolve our business problems once and for all." She sounded considerably better than she had yesterday. Maybe the simple act of taking action had renewed her spirits. As psychiatrists say, any action is better than no action.

"Unfortunately, we won't be here to have dinner with you. Sorry to have missed you last night. Tomorrow for certain, Jess. We'll have a celebratory dinner together tomorrow night."

"As I told Walter, you don't have to worry about me."

"I've arranged a tour of the island for you today, Jess. Your driver will pick you up at the

45

main house at eleven. Does that fit in with your plans?"

"Sounds fine," I said. "But you really shouldn't have gone to all that trouble. You've got enough on your plate. Please, I'll be fine on my own. I'm a big—girl." I laughed. "A grown-up woman."

"Of course you are, but you are also our special guest and dear friend. We want you to have a simply wonderful vacation; nothing but rest and relaxation. Sorry about tonight, but we'll make it up to you when we get back."

"No making up necessary," I said. "I hope your trip is a success. Best to Walter. And thanks for calling."

I ordered croissants and a pot of coffee from room service. Thomas arrived ten minutes later carrying a wicker tray with freshly cut passion flowers in a miniature navy blue porcelain vase. The tray was lined with a yellow and pale blue floral placemat. It was as visually inviting as it was tasty.

I enjoyed a leisurely breakfast on the terrace, alternating between the melt-in-your-mouth buttery croissants and the steaming, aromatic, muscular coffee. An added ingredient were the delicious "tastes" around me—the sunrise playing on the waters of Lover's Lagoon, the mellow breezes, the fragrant trees. Does the soaking in of this brand of luxury ever become boring, I wondered. I answered my question by picking up a guidebook I'd brought with me and turning to the section on tourist attractions. I found what I was looking for: the page on which local government institutions were detailed. Friends have often told me that my interest in politics would be better served by living in Washington, D.C. than Cabot Cove. But politics on a large scale hold little appeal for me. I love small-town politics, Cabot Cove's town meetings and local elections in which a dozen votes decide the winner. I've been urged to run for office back home, but have never succumbed to the temptation. I'd make a terrible elected official, and know it. Better that I remain an interested spectator and informed voter.

Whenever I travel, I always try to find a few hours to witness local government in action. The guidebook noted that sessions of the U.S. Virgin Islands' Legislature were open to the public, and that visitors to the islands were especially welcome.

"Legislature Building. An unimposing pastel green building on the harbor. It was built in 1874 as a barracks for Danish police. It is now the seat of the Virgin Islands Legislature. Previously, it served as housing for units of the United States Marine Corps, and as a public school. It is open Monday through Friday."

If the Legislature was in session, I'd ask my driver to allow me an hour to soak it in. I finished breakfast, took a shower, and headed for the pool before the sun had a chance to heat things up. My timing was good; I was the only person at the pool. After swimming enough laps to assuage my guilt over last night's caloric dinner, I returned to my room where I read until it was time to meet my driver.

His name was Peter. He was on time, neatly dressed in white slacks, colorful floral shirt, and

47

sandals, extremely courteous and, I would soon learn, talkative. He'd been an islander all his life and demonstrated admirable pride in his homeland. "Mrs. Marschalk told me to drive you to Charlotte Amalie," he said as he put the Jeep in gear. "She told me to give you lots of time to walk about the city and to shop. I'll be happy to escort you. I know the shopkeepers. Some are my cousins. I got lots of cousins. They'll give you the best deal if I'm with you."

"That sounds fine," I said from the backseat. "I would like to spend an hour at the government building down at the harbor."

He slowed down and turned. "Why do you want to do that?"

"Just because—"

"You got some kind of trouble?" he asked.

"No, I—"

"I got a cousin with the police. He's a big mon, a big shot."

"No, I don't have any trouble. Do you know if the Legislature is in session today?"

"No, ma'am, and don't really care. Politicians. They just sit and talk about nothing."

I laughed. "I know that," I said, "but I would enjoy hearing them talk, even about nothing."

"No problem, ma'am. Remember, this is the Caribbean. Everything is 'no problem.'" He was such a likable person, friendly without being overbearing, and with a knack for knowing what to say, and when to stop saying it. He must do nicely when it comes to tips.

Peter seemed to know everyone on the island. The trip was punctuated with someone waving at him, or honking their horns every few minutes.

"Cousins?" I asked.

"Yes, ma'am."

He stopped in front of a white cement house with a front porch. "That's my momma's house," he said. "I was born right inside there. So was my eleven brothers and sisters. Seven of 'em still live there with momma."

"She must be quite a woman."

"The best, ma'am. You want to come in and meet her?"

"No, thank you. That would be an imposition. Besides, I'm anxious to get to town."

"As you say." He beeped the horn, and people from inside the house came to the porch and waved. I returned the greeting as Peter roared off in the direction of Charlotte Amalie, leaving behind a cloud of dust that enveloped the porch of his birthplace.

We entered the crowded and congested capital city of Charlotte Amalie where tourists from the large cruise ships swarmed over endless vendors strung out along the dock. "Best to avoid this area," said Peter. "Not dangerous, mind you, but these guys sell junk. The best shops are up these cobblestone streets. See?" I looked in the direction he pointed. "Lots of beautiful and expensive shops up there. Good merchandise for sale. Big money but no problem, huh?"

I looked down to see what I was wearing that spoke money to Peter. My J. Crew cotton skirt and blouse spoke only comfort to me. Maybe it was my wedding ring; it looked a lot more than it had cost. Of course, from Peter's perspective, staying at Lover's Lagoon Inn said worlds about a person's net worth.

He pulled up to the curb where one of the narrow cobblestone streets began. "This is a good place for you to start your walk, ma'am. Want me to go with you?"

"No, thank you. It would bore you. I just want to stroll at my leisure, window-shop. Better if I do it alone."

"As you wish. Two hours?"

"That sounds about right. Maybe we can do some sightseeing from the Jeep this afternoon."

"At your service all day."

"Where will I meet you?" I asked.

"Over there, ma'am. Can't miss it." He pointed to a building across the street. It was neon pink. We both laughed. As I started to exit the Jeep, he said, "If you'll be looking for jewelry, ma'am, I recommend that shop." He indicated a modest storefront a few yards up the cobblestone street. A sign in front read: "LOVER'S LAGOON FINE JEWELRY."

"Your cousin's place?" I asked lightly.

"That's right. I'll tell him to be expecting you. Give you the best price, that's for sure."

"Thank you," I said. "Any other suggestions?"

"If you'll be having lunch, I recommend Rasheda's Long Look Vegetarian Restaurant. Very popular with tourists. Be sure to have a glass of sea moss."

"What is it?" I asked.

"Seaweed. But it doesn't taste like it. Much sweeter."

"I'll be sure to try it," I said. This was a time when lying was definitely the better part of valor.

I decided to put off looking at jewelry until the end of my walk. The sun was hot and so I tried to stay in the shade as I made my way through the city, my guidebook my map. There were a surprising number of churches for such a small

50

island, and a synagogue the book said was the oldest in continuous use under the American flag. I walked up a steep, narrow street known as Ninety-nine Steps for obvious reasons (I didn't count the steps as I ascended, but was convinced upon reaching the top that there were more than ninety-nine of them.) At the top was a neighborhood known as Queen's Street, and a guest house called Blackbeard's Castle, originally part of a castle supposedly the home of a notorious twentieth-century pirate named Edward Teach. How romantic. The only pirates these days seem to be elected officials. With that unkind thought, I decided to have lunch at Blackbeard's Castle. It was a good decision. My sandwich and iced tea were served on a terrace near a pool, and offered me lovely views of the city and harbor beyond.

Refreshed, I headed back down into the center of town. I had a half hour before meeting up with Peter again. I was almost to his "cousin's" jewelry store when I noticed a bookstore. Try as I might, I simply cannot pass a bookstore without stopping in.

The minute I entered the pleasant, air-conditioned shop, I was face-to-face with a rack filled with the paperback edition of my last book that had been published in hardcover a year ago. I sometimes buy a copy of my books when visiting bookstores, and decided this would be one of those times. Because it can be embarrassing to be caught purchasing a book you've written (does it hint that it isn't being bought by others?) I try to do it without being identified as the author. I was confident that my straw hat with its large, floppy brim that dipped low over my eyes, and my oversize sunglasses would do the trick.

"That will be $4.95," said the gentleman at the register. I opened my purse and handed him a five-dollar bill. He said as he gave me my change, "There you go, Mrs. Fletcher."

All I could do was laugh.

"Thought you'd sneak out without anyone recognizing you, eh?" he said, flashing a broad, friendly grin marred by badly discolored teeth. "Walter and Laurie are good friends of mine. When they told me you'd be visiting us, I stocked up."

"Well, this is a pleasant surprise," I said, offering my hand.

He took it. "My name's Justin Wall, Mrs. Fletcher. Your books are selling very well since word got around you'd be on St. Thomas. I asked Walter if you might be interested in doing an autographing session here at the store, but he came to your defense immediately, told me this was your well-deserved vacation and that nothing should interfere."

"I must thank him," I said.

"But would you sign just one for me personally? Even your initials." He smiled that smile again.

"Of course. I'd be happy to."

As I wrote, *For Justin, best wishes, Jessica Fletcher,* he said, "I have one question about this book, Mrs. Fletcher, a question that bothers me."

"Yes?" I said.

"The use of a razor as a murder weapon. Surprisingly brutal for you, isn't it? I mean, in all your previous books—at least those I've read—the means of murder are considerably more genteel. Poison, a car tampered with, perhaps a gun. But a razor. Is that to satisfy society's increasing need for violence?"

"No," I said. "I don't try to satisfy society when I write. I just felt that—well, I'm sorry it shocked you. I'll think twice before being so brutal in the future."

"You aren't offended," he said.

"Gracious, no. I appreciate such feedback. I learn from it."

He thanked me for the autographed book, leaned on the counter, and said in low tones, "Damn shame what's happening to Walter and Laurie."

"I don't know—what *is* happening to them?"

"You haven't read the paper today?"

"No."

"I just hope it's not true, and that the editors have it wrong."

"Have what wrong?" I asked.

His voice dropped even lower. "Seems there's some sort of government investigation into their inn. According to the article, Walter illegally purchased Lover's Lagoon by bribing one of our politicians, Bobby Jensen."

"That's a serious charge," I said, recalling what Walter had told me at dinner.

"The newspaper goes on to say that Walter and Laurie owe a lot of money on it, and to bad people."

"Bad people? What bad people?"

"Criminals back in the States."

I shook my head. "You're right, Mr. Wall. The editors must have it wrong. Do you have a copy of today's paper?"

"No, but they'll have one on the newsstand 'round the corner."

53

I thanked him and hurried out the door.

Sure enough, the headline on the *St. Thomas Gazette* read: "LOVER'S LAGOON INVESTIGATION LAUNCHED." A photo of Bobby Jensen ran on the front page. Walter's photo appeared where the story jumped to page three. I shoved the paper in my large straw bag. I would read it back at the hotel.

Walter and Laurie must be devastated over this, I thought. I'd sure picked a heck of a time to visit them. Did Walter's death threat have something to do with the investigation? He hadn't seemed overly concerned about it. It was good they'd gotten off the island, if even for a day. It occurred to me that because they were in Miami, they might not have seen the newspaper story. I hoped they hadn't. They had enough on their minds without having this interfere with the meeting with their attorney.

I downed a cup of ice-cold mango juice purchased from a street vendor and checked my watch. It was time to meet Peter in front of the pink building. I would pass Lover's Lagoon Fine Jewelry on the way. I wouldn't have gone in it except that I saw Peter through the window. He greeted me warmly and introduced me to his cousin, the owner.

"I have something 'specially picked out for you, Mrs. Fletcher," said the cousin. He placed a felt pad on the counter. Displayed on it was gold pendant in the shape of Lover's Lagoon.

"It's lovely," I said.

"I designed it myself," Peter's cousin said. "For you, a very special price."

And so I bought it, as well as a gold chain on which to hang it. While he attached the chain, he waxed poetic about the real Lover's Lagoon. "The most beautiful spot in the world," he said. I thought I detected a Boston accent.

"Undoubtedly true," I said, "provided you don't count the beaches of Cape Cod."

That caused him to laugh. He had grown up in Boston but returned to St. Thomas ten years ago. "You know, Mrs. Fletcher, wearing this pendant will always ensure your good fortune," he said. "It has the same mystical powers as the lagoon itself. 'Kiss her once in Lover's Lagoon, and she will be yours forever.'"

"Does it work the other way around?" I asked.

"Of course," he said. "Kiss *him* once—"

"I really must be going," I said. I was enjoying the conversation but the newspaper and its accusatory article weighed heavy in my bag. "Thank you. You've been very kind and generous. I'll wear it with pride."

The minute we got into Peter's Jeep, I pulled the paper from my bag and began to read.

"Where to?" Peter asked.

"What? Oh, sorry. Have you seen the paper today?"

"Yes, ma'am. You're referring to the story about the Marschalks."

"Yes."

"I don't know what to believe," he said sadly. "Still want to go to the Legislature Building?"

"More than ever," I answered, going back to my reading.

The article was filled with unsubstantiated charges and unattributed sources. Basically, it accused Walter and Laurie of acquiring Lover's Lagoon by virtue of having bribed Bobby Jensen to take the property off the government roll of protected land. That was nothing new. Walter had freely mentioned those charges to me at dinner.

But the writer of the piece, Adrian Woodhouse, went further. He painted Walter as an unscrupulous travel writer who was "widely known" in the travel industry to have accepted payoffs for favorable reviews.

And then the real bombshell appeared.

"Reliable sources have told this newspaper that the unsolved murder three years ago of local resident Caleb Mesreau might well be linked to the purchase by the Marschalks of Lover's Lagoon."

According to the article, Caleb Mesreau had owned a tiny portion of the land on which Lover's Lagoon Inn is now situated. Mesreau refused to sell what he owned to Walter Marschalk, or to the government. He was found murdered, his throat slit, his body jammed into a rusted oil drum and weighted to make it sink. The weights eventually came loose, and the drum and Caleb Mesreau floated to the surface. Following his disappearance, and before the discovery of his body, a deed to his land "mysteriously surfaced" and was produced by Bobby Jensen, who claimed that Mesreau's small lot had been sold to the government before his death. Because the deceased was without next of kin, and died without a will, the property clearly belonged to the government of St. Thomas, and would be included in the tract sold to the Marschalks.

Although the article did not come straight out

and accuse Walter or Jensen of having killed Mesreau, the inference was strong.

"All this because of a body of water," I muttered.

"A very special body of water, Mrs. Fletcher," Peter said. "Here we are."

We were in front of the pale green building that housed the islands' Legislature. I asked Peter to give me an hour. "Care to come with me?" I asked.

"No, ma'am. I stay away from anything government unless I'm arrested."

I smiled. "You're a wise man, Peter."

"Mrs. Fletcher."

"Yes?"

"Are you going in there because you enjoy that sort of thing, or because of the story in the newspaper?"

"Good question. Originally, just because I enjoy 'that sort of thing.' But now—well, I admit I've become curious. What do you know about this Bobby Jensen?"

"Powerful man, Mrs. Fletcher. Keeps getting elected because he knows where to spread the money around. Not a very nice man, I hear, but I don't know from my own experience. I don't vote for him."

"He doesn't give you money?"

"No, he doesn't. I'll be waiting."

A tall, lanky guard stood at the front entrance. I asked him about access to whatever government business might be going on at the moment. He shrugged his shoulders, which looked like suit hangers beneath his shoulder pads, and suggested I check in with the public affairs office.

Once inside, I decided I'd bypass Public Affairs

and simply try a few of the massive mahogany doors that opened off the wide hallway. It was eerily quiet in the building. I saw no one. I was about to choose the first door to open when I heard footsteps on the hard marble floor. A man, followed by three other men, walked quickly toward me. I recognized him immediately. It was Senator Bobby Jensen.

"Senator Jensen," I said. "My name is Jessica Fletcher. I'm a close personal friend of Walter and Laurie Marschalk." He stopped as if someone had pulled on his reins, and smiled a politician's smile. If I'd had a baby in my arms, he would have planted a kiss on it.

"Yes, Mrs. Fletcher. Welcome to sunny St. Thomas. Walter Marschalk told me you'd be visiting, and I fully intend to make it over to Lover's Lagoon before you leave."

"I'd look forward to that."

"What brings you here?" he asked, indicating the building with a nod of his head.

"I always enjoy—well, to be honest, I've just read the paper. It's a shocking series of allegations they've made about you and the Marschalks."

His face turned hard. It was a youthful face, far younger than his age. He was light-skinned, almost Caucasian. His hair was reddish blond. His clothing was expensively cut.

"We have to go," one of his aides said.

"In a minute," Jensen responded. He looked me squarely in the eye. "Are you down here writing a book about this?" he asked.

"About *this*? This scandal? Heavens, no. I'm on vacation, pure and simple."

"Come here," he said, taking my arm and

leading me to a corner where the others wouldn't hear. "Let me tell you something, Mrs. Fletcher, that you probably already know. Walter and Laurie Marschalk are two of the nicest people in the world. I treasure their friendship. Now let me tell you something you don't know. My colleagues who are calling for this absurd probe into Walter's purchase are whores. They're on Diamond Reef's pad and have been for a long time. Until today they've snuck around trying to dig up evidence to support their claims. Now, they think they have. But you read the paper. Nothing but rumors and innuendo designed to ruin innocent people like the Marschalks—and me. It's all political. Greed. Jealousy."

"I'm certainly happy to hear there's no substance to the story," I said, not quite sure what the proper response was.

"Senator!" an aide said sharply.

"Have to run, Mrs. Fletcher. Have to catch a flight to Miami. Nice meeting you. Say hello to Walter and Laurie for me."

"They're in Miami," I said. "They're due back tomorrow. What about this Mesreau character I read about?"

"Just a crazy old coot who got his throat slit by assailants unknown. I'll get over to buy you a drink before you leave the inn. That's a promise." With that he was gone, saying over his shoulder, "I've read some of your books. They're good. I like them a lot." He stopped, added, "If you need anything, anything at all, see my secretary. Room Seven. Tell her I said to give you carte blanche."

I left the building and climbed into Peter's Jeep.

"Just heard the news on the radio," he said as he started the engine.

"What news?"

"Senator Bobby Jensen resigned this afternoon over the investigation."

"I just—I just spoke with him."

"Bet it's the last we'll ever see of him on St. Thomas," said Peter. "They say he's got millions stashed away in Miami. Probably go back there and be a big-shot lawyer. Where to?"

"Home," I said, thinking of Cabot Cove.

I considered walking down to the lagoon, but a typical late afternoon rainstorm seemed imminent. The air was uncomfortably close. I went to my room, stretched out on the bed, and closed my eyes. For some reason I was hungry, famished. The sandwich at Blackbeard's Castle had been tasty but small. I got up, took a banana from the fruit basket on the wicker table, and sat on the terrace. Music by a steel drum band at Diamond Reef drifted to where I sat. They seemed to have music twenty-four hours a day. I pondered what I was about to do, which meant chewing my cheek, a bad habit that sometimes gets out of hand. Why not? I was free for dinner. I'd be dining at the inn for the rest of my stay once Walter and Laurie returned.

I found Mark Dobson's card in my purse and poised to call him, thought better of it, got Diamond Reef's number from the operator and called its restaurant directly. "I'd like to make a dinner reservation for eight this evening," I said.

"Of course. What is your room number?"

"I'm not staying at Diamond Reef. Is that a problem?"

"Not at all. How many for dinner?"

"Just myself."

"Your name?"

"Fletcher. Mrs. Fletcher."

"Splendid, Mrs. Fletcher. See you at eight."

Chapter 6

I dislike people who aren't on time, and make it a habit—no, it's really more of an obsession—to be where I'm supposed to be when scheduled. It has long been my contention that people who are chronically late are simply attention seekers; others are always waiting anxiously for the "arrival," or hovering around a tardy person whose slowness keeps a group from leaving.

That's why I was upset with myself when I arrived late for my dinner reservation at Diamond Reef. Just ten minutes late, but late is late. My excuse was that the navy blue blazer I'd chosen to wear with an aquamarine-and-white sheath was lacking a button, which I discovered on my way out the door. Ordinarily, I would have checked the evening's wardrobe well in advance. But as had become a pattern since arriving on St. Thomas, I'd fallen asleep on the terrace while reading and awoke with a start. I obviously needed an alarm clock on the terrace more than in the bedroom.

"Good evening," a petite young black woman with a cameo face asked as I stepped up to the restaurant's podium.

"I'm Mrs. Fletcher. I'm a few minutes late. My reservation was for eight."

She anxiously glanced down at the reservation book, looked at me and smiled, then scanned the book more hurriedly.

"Is there a problem?" I asked.

"Yes, there appears to be." Her voice said she was nervous. First day on a new job? "Mrs. Fletcher has already arrived," she said.

"Really?" I couldn't help but smile.

"What I mean is that Mrs. Fletcher has already—" She pointed to a table set for two in a far corner of the large, nautically appointed room, where a young woman perused a menu.

"Well," I said, "there obviously are two Mrs. Fletchers dining here this evening."

"I'm afraid we don't have—" She was interrupted by a man with skin the color of ink. He carried his white tuxedo with an air of royalty, his handsomely sculpted head held at a slight angle that gave the impression he questioned everything, and everyone. "Is there a problem?" he asked in a deep voice that did not clash with his physical bearing.

The young woman, whose nerves were now very much on edge, explained the situation.

"I see," the man said. He surveyed the dining room. Every table was taken, with the exception of a few large ones set for six and eight persons. "Unfortunately, we have only tables reserved for large parties," he said. "Would you be averse to sharing the table with your namesake?"

It wasn't what I had in mind, and I thought about returning to the inn for a solitary dinner. "I think you'd better ask the other Fletcher how she would feel about that," I said.

The maître d' strode across the room, conferred with the woman, looked back at me, and motioned. The hostess escorted me to the table. "Mrs. Fletcher, meet Mrs. Fletcher," the maître d' said. We smiled at each other and shook hands. There was a look of recognition on her face. "*The* Jessica Fletcher?" she said.

"*C'est moi,*" I said, out of character. I wasn't very good in situations in which I was recognized and usually said something silly when confronted with them. Like using a foreign phrase. I never end a conversation with "*Ciao.*"

"I thought it was you standing there," the younger woman said. The maître d' held out my chair.

"I hope you don't mind my joining you," I said. "There was a mix-up. Having the same name and all."

She introduced herself as Jennifer Fletcher. Even the same first initial, I thought. "There is a difference between us," she said. "You're *Mrs.* Fletcher. Afraid I'm a Ms."

I smiled. "Actually, I am, too. My husband is deceased, but I carry my Mrs. designation. You're allowed to do that, I'm told."

"I would hope so," she said.

Jennifer Fletcher had sun-washed shoulder-length blond hair, a tan that was copper in tone, and a dusting of freckles on her cheeks. A pretty young woman, wholesome and nicely chiseled. At first glance I'd pegged her to be in her late twenties. But closer up I reevaluated. Thirty-five, I guessed. A girlish thirty-five. I assumed she was tall, although I couldn't tell as long as she remained seated.

She giggled. "I'm expecting someone to say, 'Smile. You're on Candid Camera.'"

I took her seriously for a moment and glanced over my shoulder.

"I can't believe I'm having dinner with Jessica Fletcher," she said. "I've read some of your books. In fact, I'm reading one now. She pulled a paperback edition of one of my earlier works from her handbag. "I travel a lot. That's why I always buy paperbacks. Lighter to carry." She said it apologetically, as though there was something sinful about not buying hardcover editions of my books.

"I prefer paperbacks, too, when traveling," I said.

She became outwardly more formal, and sat erect in her chair. "I *love* your writing. I aspire to write like you. I can't believe we'll be having dinner together. This is a wonderful surprise."

"Consider the privilege mine. It's not every night I get to dine with a relative."

We both laughed.

"Are you on vacation?" I asked.

"No. I'm here as part of a travel writers' press trip to cover a conference sponsored by the Tourism Board. The conference doesn't kick off until tomorrow. Most of the other writers won't arrive until then. I decided to come a day early to give myself time to explore a little. And, between you and me, to find some time to relax. Press trips can be grueling. They schedule activities every minute of the day. The better ones try to work in some free time, but that's usually taken up returning phone calls back to the office, and going over my notes."

"A grind that probably seems like nothing but pure fun to onlookers," I said.

"Exactly."

"Sounds like a fascinating job to me. Do you work for a particular magazine or newspaper?"

"I'm senior editor at a trade magazine called *Travel Agent Magazine* back in New York. It's written for travel agents and travel consortiums. I usually write about hotels, but they sent me down here to cover the conference. I suppose I'll do a story on Diamond Reef as well. Actually, I'd like to do a story on Lover's Lagoon Inn next door. We get the word there's an investigation going on. I know the man who owns it, Walter Marschalk. He used to be a travel writer. A big-time one. I've been on a lot of press trips with him."

Although I count promptness among my virtues, I also admit to my failings. One of them is a tendency to not be completely truthful when wanting to learn something from a stranger. Not that I lie outright. It's just that I withhold certain information in order to gain the confidence of the other person, and to promote candor. That's why I didn't mention, at least at that moment, that I was Walter and Laurie Marschalk's personal friend. But I would tell Jennifer I was staying at Lover's Lagoon Inn, and did.

"How is it?" she asked.

"Extraordinary. Everything about it is exceptional."

"That's some endorsement."

We both looked up at a young man belonging to a voice that said, "Hello, Jennifer."

"Fred!" She was obviously surprised to see him. "I thought you weren't making this trip. When did you arrive?"

"I changed my mind. A few minutes ago. You could invite me to sit down."

Jennifer didn't respond. She didn't seem overly pleased at seeing this young man. I would have thought she'd have been delighted. She might have been initially impressed with my celebrity,

66

but I assumed would prefer the company of a handsome man her age.

Or younger. Fred was no older than thirty. He was beach-bum blond, handsome, tanned, and well-built, with watery pale blue eyes. Most striking to me, however, was the cruelty in those eyes. If not cruelty, a discernable lack of compassion and spark. Like so many young men these days, always brooding, pondering Lord knows what. Closed and guarded, as though to openly express emotion might prove fatal.

"Fred Capehart, this is Jessica Fletcher," Jennifer said.

"Hi," he said. "Fletcher? Same name as Jennifer."

"Yes. It caused some confusion when I—" I knew he wouldn't be interested and didn't bother finishing the story. "Been next door yet?" he asked Jennifer.

Next door? Lover's Lagoon Inn?

"No," she said coldly.

"I'm impressed. How could you stay away from *him* so long?"

Jennifer's tightly pursed lips testified to her anger. She turned and stared at the ceiling.

I surmised the "him" to which Fred Capehart had referred was Walter Marschalk, but I didn't indicate that. I simply said, "Jennifer and I were discussing Lover's Lagoon when you arrived, Fred. Have you been there?"

He'd ignored me until I asked the question. Now, he turned and said to me, "I wouldn't waste my time."

"It's very nice. I'm staying there."

He turned to Jennifer. "Let's get out of here."

"You're being rude, Fred."

"Perhaps I should—" I started to say.

"This is Jessica Fletcher, the famous mystery writer," Jennifer said.

His response was to glance at me, then return his attention to Jennifer.

"I think I'll leave you two alone for the evening," I said, picking up my bag from the floor.

"Please don't go," Jennifer said.

"No, I'm in the mood for something light from room service. A good book and early to bed. It was nice meeting you, Jennifer. I hope to see you again."

Fred reacted to my standing by getting up, too. "It was nice meeting you."

"Have a nice evening."

I paused at the manager's podium on my way out and looked back at the table. I couldn't hear what they were saying, but their body language shouted that they weren't exchanging words of endearment. "What a boring young man," I mumbled to myself as I went to the patio where dozens of couples danced to that evening's musical entertainment. It was a brilliantly clear night. The moon was full; it appeared to be ten times larger than when viewed in Cabot Cove.

I was disappointed that Jennifer and I had been interrupted. I liked her, and had looked forward to a pleasant conversation. Perhaps an illuminating conversation, too. She obviously knew Walter Marschalk pretty well, and was aware of the controversy that had erupted over his inn. I'd meant what I'd said when leaving the table. I did want to speak with her again, and would make a point of seeking her out.

I was about to leave the patio and head for

my villa when Diamond Reef's general manager, Mark Dobson, called my name and approached on his crutches. "Good evening, Mr. Dobson."

"Good evening, Mrs. Fletcher. Decided to visit us again?"

To seek asylum from Lover's Lagoon Inn? I wouldn't give him that satisfaction. "Just taking a stroll," I said.

"Feel like dinner? My treat."

"Thank you, no. I was just—no, I'm planning a quiet night in my villa. I'll have something sent up."

"The invitation's always there, Mrs. Fletcher. Read the paper today?"

"About Walter Marschalk and the charges against him? Yes, I did."

"He's in a lot of trouble."

"He's been accused of something, that's all," I said. "Accusations are easy. Proving them is something else."

Dobson laughed. "Oh, they'll prove it, Mrs. Fletcher, because the accusations are true. Trust me."

"Lovely evening, isn't it?" I said.

"Just your typical, run-of-the-mill St. Thomas night," he said. "A drink? At least let me buy you a drink."

"Thanks, but not tonight. Have a nice evening."

I returned to my villa and ordered a Caesar salad, rolls, and tea. A pervasive, free-floating anxiety settled over me. I was as fidgety as an ant, couldn't sit still. I tried reading but lost interest in the book, a first novel by a young woman from Maine who delved into her heroine's passage into adulthood too deeply for my taste. I'd started another when dinner arrived. Thomas, as unfailingly pleasant and courteous as ever, set me up on the terrace where I ate to the accompaniment of steel drums from Diamond Reef, with vocals provided by my resident tree frogs.

I thought the food and hot tea might relax me sufficiently to induce a sound sleep. It didn't happen. My body was tired from all the walking that day in Charlotte Amalie, but my mind was racing. I reread the article about Walter and the charges he'd bribed island Senator Bobby Jensen to acquire Lover's Lagoon. I didn't want to believe it. Walter was a good friend, and I counted Laurie among my favorite people. Still, otherwise nice people sometimes do not do very nice things, especially when driven in pursuit of a goal, in this case the splendiferous lagoon that was only a hundred yards from where I sat.

And I hadn't been to it yet. I went to the edge of the terrace and looked down to where it shimmered in the moonlight like black plastic. I checked my watch. It was a few minutes before midnight. A long day. Maybe it would be better to visit the lagoon in the morning, in the daylight, take my coffee there and enjoy a relaxing hour on the beach. But I couldn't resist.

I slipped into my sandals, draped a light sweater over my shoulders, and stepped outside, inhaling the lush scent of pink oleanders, whose hedges defined the small plot of grass in front of my villa. I found the beginning of a narrow dirt path lined with coconut palms and started down. It wasn't lighted very well but didn't have to be. The moon provided ample illumination.

I looked back. Everything was quiet at the main house, and in the villas; the only sign that I was not alone outside was a couple holding hands as they crossed the restaurant terrace and entered the inn.

I continued down the gentle slope in the direction of the lagoon, pausing at a point where the dirt path became an equally narrow brick walkway. It was so quiet and peaceful that I could have suffered sensory deprivation. The feeling of isolation was delicious. We all have a need to be alone at times, but find so few opportunities. Most times, we think we're alone but aren't. People may be absent, but the world is always there to intrude.

This was different. I *was* alone. And I reveled in it.

I reached the slender strip of beach and looked out over the glassy black water. A bird screeched and flew from a tree, its graceful form a fluid silhouette against a sky graced with millions of stars. It had startled me, and I let out an involuntary whoosh of air. I smiled. You never are really alone.

I took off my shoes and wiggled my toes in the talcum powder sand. The water looked inviting, but I wouldn't have ventured in for a dip even if I had worn my bathing suit. Who knew what lurked below? I've always had a reputation for being adventurous, but I pick my adventures carefully. Swimming in strange water, and without a companion, was not one for which I would opt.

I went to the water's edge and stepped in far enough to cover my bare feet. It was considerably warmer than I'd expected. Still it was refreshing. I slowly meandered the length of the beach, keeping my feet in the water. I felt childlike. And then lonely. What a perfect spot to share with someone. With a lover. Lover's Lagoon. "Kiss in it, and you'll enjoy a long and happy life together." A lovely thought. My thoughts went to George Sutherland, my friend with Scotland Yard in London. We hadn't had the time in London to get to know each other well. But he had expressed, with awkward charm, warm feelings for me before I left England for home, and our correspondence had been relatively frequent and personal.

As I continued my aimless stroll, I also thought of my deceased husband. We'd shared many loving moments together in beautiful, exotic places like Lover's Lagoon. I missed him as strongly at that moment as I did the day he died. I guess that's what happens when you spend so many happy years with a man. You never stop missing. And hurting, although the hurt finds places to hide as time goes by.

I stopped, looked up at the sky, and said to whomever might be up there, "Thank you for this wonderful life of mine." I felt a chill, but not because of the temperature. I was chilled with pleasure. The problem of Walter and the charges against him hadn't accompanied me to the lagoon. There weren't any problems down here. I decided I would end each evening on St. Thomas with a walk on this tiny beach because I knew that if I did that, no matter what else might happen, my vacation would be a success.

I had to stop because the beach ended at a bank of trees, beneath which was a low cover of prickly shrubbery. I sensed that another beach continued on the other side but wasn't accessible except by swimming. I turned to retrace my steps, stopped, lifted my right foot, and examined its sole. I'd stepped on something soft. A jellyfish? Seaweed? Laurie had cautioned me to not step on, or touch certain things on the beach. "They sting," she'd said. "A few can make you sick."

I turned my body so as to not block light from the moon, and leaned over to see what had been beneath my foot. It couldn't be. A hand? A human hand?

And then I saw the body to which the hand was attached. It was half in the water, its lower extremities covered by the low growth. The face was partially submerged, the eyes open wide and looking up. A pool of blood lay on top of the lagoon's water, the crimson mixture running in and out of the open mouth.

"Oh, my God," I whispered. I bent further to reaffirm the identity of the body, and almost lost my balance in the process. The hand, the face, the lifeless body belonged to Walter Marschalk. And then I saw the gaping, oozing gash across his throat that reached from ear to ear.

I straightened up and jammed my fist against my mouth to stifle a scream that threatened to come out. It took me a few moments to gather enough composure to leave the beach in search of someone to tell. I no longer felt childlike. I felt disgustingly grown-up.

Yes, Walter, I would take any death threat seriously.

Chapter 7

"Good morning, Mrs. Fletcher. Sorry to be calling so early." It was six-fifteen. Another morning of beating the birds out of bed. "This is Detective Calid. We talked last night."

"Last night" was only a few hours ago. I'd given a brief statement to the detective after having reported Walter's murder, and asked if I might get a few hours' sleep before undergoing any questioning. He readily agreed, and as traumatic as my discovery had been, I was asleep in minutes.

"I need to talk to you, Mrs. Fletcher. May we come to your room?"

What I wanted to do was pull the sheets over my head and suggest we get together twelve hours from now. But that was obviously out of the question. I sat up in bed, rubbed my eyes, and prepared to begin another vacation day. "Can you give me fifteen minutes?" I asked. "Enough time for a fast shower and to get dressed?"

"Of course. I appreciate your cooperation."

I stood under the shower and tried to pull together my thoughts, especially the sequence of events from the time I'd found Walter's body. I'd awoken the inn's assistant manager and asked him to call the police. They seemed to take forever to arrive, although I suppose it always seems that way when you desperately want them to be there. Eventually, two vehicles pulled up in the driveway, one a marked patrol car, the other without any official indications. There were four policemen, including Detective Calid.

Calid had been extremely courteous and sensitive. He realized how shaken I was and didn't probe for, nor give any gruesome descriptions. I waited in the dining room while he and his colleagues went down to Lover's Lagoon to examine the body. Calid returned a half hour later, confirmed that Walter was, indeed, dead, and commented that it was his guess that the weapon had been a straight razor. "Could be something else I suppose," he'd added, "but it was a very sharp instrument."

The wait in the dining room gave me a chance to clear my mind and to get over the physical tremors I'd been experiencing. "Any idea how long he's been dead?" I asked, not certain whether it was my place to ask such a question.

Calid scrutinized me. "I know you are a famous author of murder mysteries, Mrs. Fletcher," he said. "I imagine you have a lot of questions to ask me."

"Oh, no, not at all. And if I'm out of line, just say so."

He nodded, said, "The coroner will have to determine the time of death. If you are wondering about a motive, it wasn't robbery. The deceased had more than two hundred dollars in his pockets."

Remarkably, no one at the inn knew how to reach Laurie. She'd left no hotel name, no number. All they knew was that she'd gone to Miami, and was due back the next day.

"I thought Walter was going with her," I said to the assistant manager.

"So did I," he replied.

When I'd returned to my villa for a few hours' rest, they still hadn't been able to contact her.

I'd just emerged from the shower and was drying off when the phone rang. Conveniently, there was an extension on the wall next to the sink.

"Hello, Jessica." It was Laurie.

"Oh, Laurie. I'm so sorry." It dawned on me, too late, that she might not be aware of Walter's death. But that wasn't the case.

"The police told me last night. They got hold of my attorney in Miami. He knew how to reach me. I'm back in St. Thomas. I chartered a plane as soon as I received the news."

"I'm glad they found you."

"Jessica, I understand that you were the one who found Walter's body. Would you tell me about it? Please. I feel so guilty not having been there."

"Being here wouldn't have helped anything," I said, not sure I meant it. If she had been, it might have altered Walter's schedule, kept him away from the lagoon. Providing, of course, that he was murdered there. He could have been killed elsewhere, his body brought to the lagoon.

No, he was killed there. I didn't have any doubts about that.

I was tempted to ask why Walter hadn't accompanied her to Miami, but decided it wasn't the time or circumstance to begin probing. There would be plenty of time for such questions when we were together.

I started to fill Laurie in on how I happened upon Walter's body when there was a loud knock on my door. "Laurie, please hold on. The police are here to question me."

"I know. They just left me. I'll see you later?"

"Of course. If you need any help with anything, Laurie, funeral arrangements, contacting people back home, just yell." Laurie and Walter never had children, and I knew that both sets of parents were deceased.

"Thanks, Jessica. You're a real friend. I'm just sorry this happened while you were here. That you had to discover the body is—"

"Enough of that, Laurie."

There was another knock on the door, this time louder. "Just know I'm here for you, Laurie. And again, I'm so very sorry."

She was openly crying now. "What kind of vicious animal could have done this to my husband?" she managed between sobs. "I need answers."

"I'm sure you'll have them," I said.

"Mrs. Fletcher, please open the door!" an impatient voice shouted. I could envision them kicking in the door any second. "Hold on, Laurie, while I answer the door."

"No. I'll let you go, Jess. Talk to you later."

"Coming," I yelled as I threw on the clothes I'd worn the previous night, which conveniently hung on a chair next to my bed. I opened the door for Detective Calid, and another plain-clothes detective who'd not been present last night. Calid, who'd been up all night, didn't seem any worse for wear. His beige silk suit looked as though it had just come from the cleaners. I noted he'd changed his shirt. It was now pale blue. Last night it was white.

He was not a handsome man by most definitions, but his pleasantness added a physical attractiveness that could not be measured. He was heavyset bordering on portly, with wide shoulders and an expansive chest. He'd lost his hair on top, and what was left on his temples was close-cropped and flecked with gray. I was certain of one thing. Despite his amiable facade, he was a man to be reckoned with. Fools and liars need not apply.

While Calid and I went to the terrace and sat at the table, the other detective, who'd been introduced as Detective Moss, prowled the living room, his eyes darting in every direction as though expecting to find a bloody razor and written confession on top of the TV. What he did find, to my embarrassment, was a disheveled room. By the time I'd returned to it last night, I simply flung my clothing on the nearest piece of furniture. Moss was considerably younger than Calid, which I suppose explained his aggressive behavior.

"Mrs. Fletcher, you were most gracious last night, considering the awful scene you discovered. I know that Walter Marschalk was a good friend."

"Yes, he was. His wife, too. We were neighbors in my hometown of Cabot Cove. That's in Maine."

A broad smile crossed his face. "I know it well," he said.

"You do?"

"Because of you. You might say you've put Cabot Cove on the map."

"I'm flattered."

"I'm sorry to have to subject you to questioning this morning, but I must."

"I understand."

"Moss! Out here." His young assistant came

to the terrace, joined us at the table, and pulled out a stenographer's pad and a pen.

"You discovered the body at approximately midnight," Calid said. "Is that correct?"

"Yes. Approximately. I know I left my villa a few minutes before midnight. It took me a few minutes to walk down to the lagoon. I strolled the beach for, say, ten minutes. That's when I found Walter. Yes, a little after midnight."

"Fine. Prior to going to Lover's Lagoon, you were—?"

"I was—let's see. I'd spent the day sightseeing in Charlotte Amalie. I napped late in the afternoon, then went next door to Diamond Reef where I had an eight-o'clock dinner reservation."

"You arrived at eight?"

"Yes. Well, not exactly. I was a few minutes late. I was wearing—it's irrelevant."

"I'm afraid nothing is irrelevant where murder is concerned."

"I suppose not." I recounted the tale of my lost button and of sewing it back on my blazer. Moss wrote as I spoke.

"You met people there?" Calid asked. "Friends?"

"No. I was dining alone. But when I got there I discovered that—a silly thing." He cocked his head. "I know," I said. "Nothing is irrelevant." I told him of the mix-up in names and how I'd ended up joining Jennifer Fletcher.

"Quite a coincidence," he said.

"Yes, it was. As Ms. Fletcher said, she expected us to be on *Candid Camera* any moment."

He chuckled. "One of my favorite shows."

"Mine, too, although I go back to when it was *Candid Microphone*."

He grunted, consulted a yellow legal pad on which he'd made a series of notes, and looked up at me with an expression that said he was waiting. I didn't know what else to offer, so I said nothing.

"You had dinner with this Jennifer Fletcher," he said.

"Yes. Not exactly. You see—someone joined us before we got to have dinner."

"Her name?"

"It was a he. Name was Fred Capehart, as I recall. Our introduction was cursory at best."

"And so you had dinner with Ms. Fletcher and this Fred Capehart."

"No. I decided to come back here and have dinner in my room."

"And?"

"And that's what I did."

Moss continued to write down what I said.

"It sounds as though you left dinner rather abruptly," Calid said.

"That's true."

"Why?"

"I felt that Ms. Fletcher and Mr. Capehart wished to have dinner together, and alone."

"What made you think that?"

"They're young—relatively—and—"

"Yes?"

"There seemed to be some tension between them. I felt it was prudent to leave."

"What sort of tension?"

"I really don't know."

But I did know. Should I tell him I suspected there was a conflict between them over Walter

80

Marschalk? I'd only surmised it. Capehart hadn't used the name. But he had indicated it had to do with "next door," which I translated into Lover's Lagoon Inn. The "him" to whom he referred *could* have been Walter. Jennifer had been discussing him when the sullen Capehart joined us.

"No idea what caused this 'tension?' "

I shook my head. It was something I'd pursue the next time I made contact with Jennifer.

"What time did you leave the table at Diamond Reef?"

"Nine. No later than that. Service was very slow. We hadn't even been served a drink or appetizer."

"I've heard service is slow there," Calid said. "You came directly back here?"

"Yes."

"And intended to go to Lover's Lagoon?"

"No. I intended to have a light dinner, read a book, and get to bed early. But I was restless after eating and decided to visit the lagoon. I hadn't been down there since arriving on Sunday."

"Did you know Walter Marschalk would be there?" Detective Moss asked.

"Of course not," I said. "It was my understanding that he'd flown to Miami with his wife and would be gone overnight."

Moss's sour expression proclaimed that he was skeptical of my answer. I looked to Calid, who smiled and resumed the questioning after thrusting Moss with a sharp glare. "Had you spent much time with the deceased since arriving on Sunday?" he asked.

"No, unfortunately. He was very busy.

Distracted with business. We had dinner together Sunday night."

"With Mr. and Mrs. Marschalk?"

"No. She was having dinner in Charlotte Amalie. A business dinner I believe."

"So you and the deceased dined together, alone."

"That's right."

"Did he seem unduly upset about anything?"

"No."

"That would be most unusual," Calid said.

"Why?" I asked.

"Considering the trouble he's in of late."

"He did mention that," I said. "But he didn't seem overly upset about it. The newspaper story hadn't appeared yet."

"He made many enemies," Calid said matter-of-factly.

"I wouldn't know about that."

"Did you meet his partner, Mr. Webb?"

"Yes, I did. He joined us at dinner."

"It was a pleasant threesome?"

"Yes. Until—"

Again, that look that asked for more.

"They got into an argument—no, more of a mild disagreement over promoting the inn."

"A mild disagreement," Moss said slowly as he wrote.

"They fought," Calid said.

"That's your choice of words."

"They resolved their differences over dinner?"

"No. As a matter of fact, they left the table."

"Not a terribly gracious way to treat a guest— as well as a good friend."

"I didn't mind. As I said, Walter had a lot of business details on his mind."

"Where did they go?" Calid asked. "Mr. Marschalk and Mr. Webb."

"I don't know. I saw them walking together outside and—"

"In the direction of the lagoon." He said it, didn't ask it.

"That's correct."

"Did you see them again after that?"

"Yes. I mean I saw Walter Marschalk again. He returned, and we continued our dinner together."

"Mr. Webb?"

"No. I did not see him again."

"Mr. Webb has left the island," said Calid. "He flew to Miami on the early flight this morning."

"I'm sure he'll return when he hears about the murder."

"I assume he will. Anything else you have to offer, Mrs. Fletcher? You've been very kind to allow us to question you after so little sleep."

"I can't think of anything else to tell you."

Calid stood, which prompted Moss to do the same. Calid twisted his spine against a pain in his lower back. "Not as young as I used to be," he said, laughing that warm, gentle, guttural laugh of his.

"If you manage to go back in time, Detective Calid, I'd appreciate hearing how you did it."

"You'll be the first to know," he said. To Moss: "Come on. It's time we left this lovely lady alone."

When they reached the door, Calid turned and said, "You'll be staying with us a bit longer I assume."

"Yes. Mrs. Marschalk will need a friend."

83

"Good. I would like the option of speaking with you again, Mrs. Fletcher."

Somehow, it came out as more of an order than a request. I said, "I'll be here for as long as Mrs. Marschalk needs me."

"Fine. In the meantime, try to relax and enjoy our island. It's a shame this incident intrudes upon your vacation. If I can be of any service, please don't hesitate to call upon me." He dropped his card on a small table next to the door and left, his assistant close behind.

Chapter 8

I'd been strangely calm during my questioning by Detective Calid and his young associate. But now that they were gone, I suffered a case of nerves. My hand trembled as I poured a glass of bottled water from the villa's mini-bar, and my heart's tempo increased to a spirited march beat. I went to the terrace, leaned on the railing, and looked down on Lover's Lagoon, where policeman raked and sifted sand through screening held taut by a wooden frame.

It was real. It *had* happened. Walter Marschalk had been murdered, his throat slit, his dream of owning a Caribbean inn pilfered from him with one swift movement of a sharp instrument. The manner in which he'd been killed made it all the more horrific. What fiend would do such a thing to another human being? Too many people was the depressing answer I gave to my rhetorical question.

I was about to go inside to change into something fresh when Thomas appeared. "Good morning, Mrs. Fletcher," he said.

"Good morning," I said. Strange how we automatically say "good morning" no matter what mayhem goes on about us.

"Might I get you something for breakfast?" he asked.

"Thank you, no. I—well, I suppose I should eat something. The usual? Croissant and coffee?"

"Yes, ma'am."

"Oh, and could I please have the newspapers?" The inn had stateside papers flown in each day. You didn't always get them the day they were published, but it was nice to have the news even twenty-four hours late.

"Of course," he said in his sweet way.

I'd changed by the time he returned, pulling white slacks, scoop-neck red cotton shirt, and sandals from the closet without much thought or conviction. Wardrobe had been rendered irrelevant by the grisly event of the previous evening. Thomas set the table on the terrace. I waited for him to mention Walter's death. That he didn't was no surprise. Thomas was a man who knew his place, as it were. His purpose was to serve, not to raise an unpleasant issue. So I raised it. "Terrible what happened last night to Mr. Marschalk," I said.

He replied without turning from his task, "I would certainly agree with that, Mrs. Fletcher."

"Do you—do you have any ideas who might have done it?" I asked.

"Me?" His smile was small. "Oh, no, ma'am. I would have no idea about that. That's what I told the police."

"Did they question you last night?"

"First thing this morning when I came on duty. Five o'clock."

"Is that the first you'd heard about it?" I asked.

His smile was now gone. Replacing it was a furrowed brow and lips pursed tightly together. He did not respond.

"Thank you," I said when he'd finished setting up breakfast.

"Yes, ma'am." He left quickly.

I took a few halfhearted nibbles of the croissant,

sipped my coffee, and focused on what had happened, and what might be in store. It occurred to me that the wisest thing I could do was leave St. Thomas. But I'd meant what I'd told Detective Calid. I would be available to help Laurie in any way I could, and until she no longer needed me. Packing up would be to abandon a dear friend in dire need. But the temptation was there. The vacation was over, no matter how many days I stayed on what had been an idyllic Caribbean island. Nothing idyllic about it anymore. Murder tends to do that to otherwise pleasant places.

It was too soon for any mention of Walter's death in the papers. But I was curious to see if the local press had followed up on the investigation into Walter's ownership of Lover's Lagoon Inn. It hadn't. Of course, the local papers were weeklies. It would take time for them to develop the story and to publish it. At least Laurie wouldn't have to deal with that this day.

I'd just about finished going through the newspapers when the phone rang. It was Laurie. "Holding up?" I asked.

"What's the alternative? Every time I'm about to give in, I think of what Walter would say. He wouldn't like it, so I don't."

"I understand. I'm showered, dressed, and have had breakfast. What can I do?"

"Nothing at the moment, but I would enjoy lunch together. By then most of the guests will have checked out. They're already starting to leave. Some are asking for refunds. I suppose I can't blame them. We don't promise murders in our brochure. Just relaxation in the sun and gourmet meals. By lunch I'll need a solid shoulder and clear head to lean on. How about my office?

87

I couldn't bear the dining room. Enough of the 'I'm so sorrys' already."

"Wherever you say. Noon?"

"Noon." She gave forth a bitter laugh. "Here you are asking what you can do for me. You're a guest. What can *we* do for *you*?"

"Make me useful. I'll be in the villa all morning. Call if you need me. Otherwise I'll stay out of your way."

I brought a pad of paper and a pen to the terrace and started making notes. I'm an inveterate list maker. I can't function without lists. I suppose I sometimes go overboard, creating lists *of* lists, much to the amusement of certain friends back in Cabot Cove. The psychologists claim that those who need lists have an untidy mind, and use lists to keep the mental clutter in-check. If they're right, so be it. All I know is that making lists provides me with a certain comfort level, which is all that matters.

I jotted down in my own brand of shorthand everything that had happened leading up to my discovery of Walter's body:

>> Laurie well-known—no ticket from cop at airport—on verge of tears—business problems—bookings down—mentioned political intrigue and corruption.

>> Dinner with Walter—looked haggard—Laurie having "business" dinner in town—claimed man at table was a spy for Diamond Reef—DR wants Lover's Lagoon—DR claiming Walter bribed politico friend Bobby Jensen—Nasty note threatening Walter's life—Partner Chris Webb joins us—argues

with Walter—they leave—Walter returns—points out young employee about to be fired—I decide to go to DR for nitecap.

>> DR big, active place—young people—Mark Dobson GM—nasty things to say about LL—travel writers confab coming up—invite me to join them.

>> Next A.M.—Walter fires employee outside my window—Laurie calls—she and Walter going to Miami to meet attorney—coming back next day—toured Charlotte Amalie—Newspaper story about investigation into LL—Bobby Jensen—bought LL pendant—Caleb Mesreau murdered—owned piece of LL land—Walter termed unscrupulous (take money for favorable reviews)—Jensen claims pol investigating LL paid by DR—Find out from driver Jensen just resigned—decide to have dinner at DR.

>> Mix-up with name (Jennifer Fletcher)—Fred Capehart arrives—nasty comment to Jennifer about Walter (my assumption it was Walter)—Jennifer have affair with Walter???? (another J.F. assumption)—DR GM Mark Dobson says accusations against Walter and LL true—I go to lagoon—find Walter's body—Didn't go to Miami—Chris Webb leaves first thing that A.M.—Razor the weapon??

I started a second list, this one headed "To Do."

>> Call Jennifer Fletcher.

>> Consider accepting Dobson's invitation to join travel writers for dinner.

>> Confirm Jensen resigned.

>> Lunch with Laurie. Ask about Chris Webb. Why Walter didn't go to Miami. Dismissed employee. Bobby Jensen.

It occurred to me as I wrote that I was injecting myself into the mystery surrounding Walter's murder as an unofficial investigator. It's happened too many times in the past to come as a surprise. Maybe it's genes. Maybe it's the result of having plotted and written too many murder mystery novels during my career. Maybe it's because a close friend had been brutally slain, and I wouldn't rest until I knew the how and why of it. My reasons were as obscure as my compulsion was strong.

Before I knew it, the morning was about to become afternoon and I was minutes away from lunch with Laurie. I literally had one foot out the door when the phone rang. I hurried back inside and answered it. "Hello, Mrs. Fletcher? Jessica?"

"Yes, this is Jessica Fletcher."

"Hi. This is Jennifer Fletcher. We met last night at the Diamond Reef."

"Of course," I said. "Hard to forget someone with your own name." I was glad she'd called. It's always satisfying to be able to cross an item off a "To Do" list.

"I just heard what happened last night, Mrs. Fletcher. Do you have a minute?"

I didn't but said, "Yes."

"Actually, I need more than a minute. Could

90

we possibly get together later today. This afternoon?"

"Yes, I think we could do that. Four o'clock?"

"I'm supposed to be attending a conference on tourism, but considering the circumstances—"

"Why don't you come to my room at Lover's Lagoon. I'm in Villa Number Ten."

"No," she said. "I mean, I'd rather not come to—would you please come to my room at Diamond Reef? I'm in twelve-oh-two."

"I'll be there at four."

"Thank you so much, Mrs. Fletcher. I have to go." She was whispering now, and I heard a male voice in the background. She abruptly hung up.

I assumed the male voice belonged to Mr. Pleasant, Fred Capehart. I hoped he wouldn't be with her at four. Then again, maybe I'd learn more from him than from her. No sense pondering it now. I'd find out when I got there.

I left my room and headed for the main building, which housed both Laurie and Walter's offices. The door to Laurie's office was closed. I knocked. No one answered. I knocked again. "Laurie? It's Jessica."

Still no response.

I walked into the small lobby where Laurie was behind the desk. Couples milled about. I saw what she'd meant. They were checking out, and some of them were vocal and loud. "I don't want a check sent to me," a man said. "I want my refund now." A woman, whose leathery skin attested to a sunbathing addiction—her face looked like a purse—said loudly, "To allow someone to have his throat slit within yards of our room is disgraceful." Her husband added, "You'll hear from our attorney."

91

Laurie glanced at me and forced a weak smile. My heart went out to her. Surely, these people knew it had been her husband who'd been murdered. The insensitivity of some people never ceases to amaze, and disgust me. "A few minutes," Laurie mouthed to me.

"Take your time," I said, wandering from the lobby and down a narrow corridor off which Walter's office opened. A bronze plaque with his name testified that he'd once been vibrant—and alive.

As I approached, a tall, young black man in a black suit, white shirt, and black tie was knocking at the office door. He held an envelope in one hand. He sensed my presence and turned. "May I help you with something?" I asked.

"Not unless you're related to this guy." He shoved a Polaroid photo of Walter at me. "His name is Walter Marschalk."

"No, I'm not related to him. But I am a close friend."

"I have papers to serve on him. I'm a process server. Do you know where he is?"

What now? I wondered. Poor Walter. Even death didn't guarantee him peace. Who could be suing him? The Diamond Reef? I knew one thing. I was going to do my best to get ahold of those papers before Laurie did. That's all she needed at this moment. I wasn't sure what the laws for serving people were in St. Thomas, but no one would arrest me for a momentary indiscretion. Would they?

"Look," I said, "I'll make sure Mr. Marschalk gets this." I pointed to the envelope the young man held firmly in a clenched hand. "As I told you, I'm a very close friend. We're practically related." I wished I'd stretched the truth in the first place and claimed that we were.

I expected to have to press the argument, but I didn't. He simply said, "All right," and handed the envelope to me. "Sign there," he said. I suppose he didn't get paid until he'd delivered the papers and had a signature to prove it. I signed at the *X*. He walked away.

I examined the envelope but its contents were securely sealed inside. I was about to hold it up to the light when Laurie came up behind. "Jessica, sorry for the delay." I quickly shoved the envelope into my straw bag, turned, and gave her a hug. "What a mess," she said.

"I saw," I said. "Some people are so rude."

"I know. In a way I'm glad to see them go. I got tired of answering questions. Let them have their damn money back."

"I know how you feel."

"Well, let's have that lunch I promised." She led me back through the lobby and to her office. "My chef couldn't get out of bed this morning," she said over her shoulder. "Not that there's anyone left to cook for except me, and you. That old saying, 'Good help is hard to find,' is the national anthem in the Caribbean. Doesn't matter. I took care of things in the kitchen."

She unlocked her office door, and we went in. "Sit down, Jess. I'll be just a minute." She pointed to a red wooden straight-back chair next to her desk, and left.

Her office was small but tastefully decorated. Framed photographs and drawings of food rivaled rows of cookbooks for wall space. Two huge color photos dominated the wall behind her desk. One was of several bulbous, ripe tomatoes and brilliant green scallions. The other featured an immense, red freshly cooked lobster sitting in a vivid yellow pool of drawn butter. I wished I'd finished my croissant.

She returned. "Sorry. Lunch will be up in a minute." She sat behind her desk, removed the baseball cap she wore, and directed a stream of air at a strand of hair that had fallen over her forehead.

"You amaze me," I said. "You just seem to keep going, like that battery bunny on TV."

"Like I said, the alternative is worse."

"I've been admiring the photographs, Laurie. They're beautiful. I guess I never stopped to think of food as being worthy of art. I was wrong."

"The photographer is a good friend of ours. Of mine now, I suppose. He's world famous for his food photography." She idly picked up a stack of mail from her desk and perused it.

I got up and looked at a bookshelf on which antique cookbooks were displayed. One caught my eye: *Maine Cooking*. I was about to pull it from the shelf when there was a knock on the door. "Come in," Laurie said. Thomas wheeled in a cart with our lunch. "Hope you don't mind I ordered for both of us," Laurie said, still examining her mail. "Shrimp salads and vichyssoise. The shrimp is absolutely the freshest. And the cocktail sauce is special, my own spicy mango sauce. I know you'll like it."

I sat at the table and waited for Laurie to join me. She was still involved with the mail, and seemed strangely detached from everything, everyone at that moment. A defense against the intense pain I knew she must be suffering? What other answer could there be for her enigmatic calm, her seeming oblivion to the fact that her husband had just been brutally murdered, her guests were exiting en masse, and the inn that represented their life's dream was under pressure from many fronts: political, legal, and certainly financial.

She dropped a fistful of mail, looked at me, and smiled. "I'm sorry, Jess. My mind keeps betraying me." She joined me at the table where Thomas stood stoically. "Thank you, Thomas," Laurie said. "I'll call you when we're done."

"Yes, ma'am. Are we expecting any arrivals today?"

Laurie frowned. "Two couples scheduled to check in, I think. *If* they haven't heard about the additional recreation we're providing these days." She laughed ruefully. "Murder mystery weekends. I understand they're quite popular now," she said. "Well, Jess, let's eat." Thomas backed from the office and closed the door.

Her demeanor had me on edge. If she'd been one thing only—sad, depressed, angry—I would have felt more comfortable. But she was mercurial, shifting rapidly from mood to mood. I wasn't being judgmental. When I lost my husband, I, too, found myself being pulled by conflicting moods and needs. And, of course, I hadn't had the additional pressure of attempting to salvage a failing business that was buffeted from all sides. I decided that I was being selfish. I wanted her to behave in a way that suited me. I wanted her to be tearful and morose, which would have made my task easier.

I remembered the legal notice in my bag, forced it from my mind, tasted my vichyssoise, smiled, and said, "It's excellent, Laurie."

95

"Glad you approve," she said. "I made it myself. Therapy. I can get lost in cooking. The world and all its nastiness disappears."

"Writing does it for me. When I'm into an especially challenging murder scene, I—" Laurie glanced at me and smiled. "I'm sorry," I said. "Sometimes my mind goes on vacation but my mouth works overtime."

"Nothing to be sorry about, Jess. Walter's murder is a fact. Reality. I'm beginning to be able to view it that way and concentrate on what needs to get done. The biggest problem at the moment is handling the press queries. They're starting to come in. I think the public relations people call it 'damage control.' Putting a positive spin on a very negative story."

"I suppose you have to deal with that," I said. "Judging from the people I saw in the lobby, business is already suffering."

"And bound to get worse." She took a few spoons of vichyssoise, sat back, raised her thin arms above her shoulders, and rested her hands on top of her head. The bags under her eyes, and a hasty job of applying makeup revealed her fatigue.

"I can't believe he's gone," she said, looking up at the ceiling. "I know it's a fact, as I said. I accept that. But part of me doesn't. A bad dream. I expect Walter to come through the door any time now. Only I know he won't." She closed her eyes tightly against tears.

"You never get over that," I said. "Expecting someone you love to walk through the door even when—anything new with the investigation?"

She shook her head. "No. I doubt if they'll come up with Walter's murderer. Not that the police here are any less efficient than anywhere else. Detective Calid has quite a reputation. He's studied all over the world, even with the FBI in the States. It's just that a random killing like this makes it impossible to resolve. No motive. Just a mentally unbalanced native."

"Are you sure about that?" I asked.

"What else? Neither Walter nor I know anyone capable of such brutality. It had to be a local."

"It wasn't robbery," I offered. "Detective Calid said Walter had a lot of cash in his pocket."

"I'd feel better if it had been a robbery. At least some poor person would have a few bucks for his trouble."

Since I couldn't suggest that Laurie eat her vichyssoise before it got cold, I ignored the food and said, "I find it interesting that the weapon was probably a straight razor. Walter was one of the few men I knew who still used such an old-fashioned type of razor to shave. It was sort of a running gag in Cabot Cove. Remember? Seth and Mort always gave him such a ribbing about it."

Laurie grinned. I was glad I'd reminded her of something amusing from yesteryear. "Walter swore by that razor," she said. "He always said to me, 'Old-fashioned or not, it's the best way to get the job done.' Ironic, isn't it?"

I remembered a time as we sat there when Walter arrived at a party wearing a bandage on his chin. When I asked what had happened, he told me he'd slipped while shaving. "I'll probably end up slitting my own throat one of these days," he'd said, laughing. It was a grim recollection that I chose not to share with Laurie.

Nor did I mention the use of a razor as a murder

weapon in my last novel, whose paperback copies were prominently displayed in Justin Wall's bookstore in Charlotte Amalie.

"Well, enough of this," Laurie said. "We have to eat, and I intend to." We finished our soup and the plump, juicy shrimp. During our meal, and the conversation that accompanied it, the phone rang numerous times. Laurie ignored the calls, said they were being answered by the assistant manager at the desk. An answering machine in her office went into action when the assistant was slow to pick up, its faint outgoing message, and the beginnings of incoming ones barely audible. "I told him not to disturb us," she said.

"I would never have thought to put mango in cocktail sauce," I said. "It adds an unusual flavor. Delicious."

"Thanks. That's what cooking is all about for me. Experimentation. Walter was my best guinea pig. He has—had a good palate. And he was honest. If he didn't like something I'd concocted, he told me."

She told whomever was knocking to come in. It was the assistant manager, a young man named Howard whose light skin testified to mixed parentage. "I really need you, Mrs. Marschalk," he said after greeting me. "I don't know how to handle all the calls from the press. New York is on the line, and I have a London journalist on hold."

"Looks like I'd better get back in the saddle, Jess." She got up and dialed for Thomas to remove the lunch table.

"Don't worry about me," I said. "Mind if I stay here awhile and browse your cookbooks?"

"Be my guest. Take them with you to your room."

"I might do that. And remember, Laurie, as long as I'm here I want to be of help."

"I certainly won't forget," she said, kissing me on the cheek. "Funny, but I wish the funeral would take place. Sort of put him, and *it* to rest in a sense. The police won't release the body until they're done investigating."

"Will the funeral be back in Cabot Cove?" I asked.

"No. Walter wanted to be buried right here, near Lover's Lagoon. I'm checking local ordinances now."

She was about to leave when I asked, "What about Mr. Webb, your partner? I understand he flew back to the States early this morning."

"Yes, he did." She opened the door and was gone.

I was left in the office with thoughts of the day my husband died, a growing list of questions about Walter's murder, and, of course, the legal papers in my straw bag. I had no business accepting them from the process server. My temptation was to simply lay the envelope on the desk and forget I'd ever seen it. But that would put Laurie in an awkward position. I'd legally taken possession of it, and for a dead man to boot. I had an obligation to do something with the papers. I was being too protective of Laurie, I decided. She appeared to be capable of juggling myriad problems at once. Some silly lawsuit against Walter probably wouldn't amount to much, not in the overall scope of things.

I've never enjoyed placing myself in moral and ethical quandaries. It can happen so fast. You take a simple action—in this case accepting the envelope from the process server without thinking—and you're then faced with the ramifications of that simple, well-meaning action.

I took *Maine Cooking* down from the shelf, opened it on my lap so that there would be a prop of sorts should Laurie suddenly reappear, removed the envelope from my bag, carefully unsealed it (which was easy since it had come partially open on its own), and removed the papers it contained. I read the first couple of lines twice to make sure I had read them right. I had. My assumption was correct. Walter was being sued.

By Laurie.

For a divorce.

Chapter 9

I avoided the lobby on the way back to my villa because I didn't want to confront Laurie. I wasn't sure I could look her in the eye.

She obviously knew divorce papers were about to be served upon Walter. Yet she'd made a point of telling me that the marriage was solid, and that it was only business that was suffering. Not that she had any obligation to share with me her marital problems. But considering the circumstances, a modicum of candor would have been appreciated.

Why hadn't she put a stop to the service of the papers the minute she knew of Walter's murder? Probably too late. Even more probable was that she simply never thought of it in the confusion that reigned during the twenty-four hours following the discovery of his body.

The irony of the situation wasn't lost on me as I poured myself a glass of mango juice from an icy pitcher that had been placed in my room. Whatever Laurie had to pay to institute divorce proceedings against her husband was wasted money. No need for a divorce now. Walter's death saw to that.

I also realized that I no longer needed to worry about having intercepted the papers from the process server. Walter's death saw to that, too.

I placed the envelope beneath a neat pile of clothing in a dresser drawer. I wasn't sure what I would eventually do with the envelope and its contents. Probably throw them away. But I didn't want to do it just yet. There was always the possibility that Laurie would find out I was the one who'd signed for them, and would want them back. In the meantime, they would remain securely in the drawer.

I was in the midst of changing clothes for my four-o'clock meeting with Jennifer Fletcher at Diamond Reef when the phone rang. "Long distance for you, Mrs. Fletcher," the inn's switchboard operator said. "Please hold." A moment later the familiar voice of Dr. Seth Hazlitt came on the line. "Jessica. Seth here."

"Hello, Seth. What a nice surprise." There was a slight delay on the line, which had us stepping on each others' words.

"I just got the news about Walter Marschalk," he said.

"Yes," I sighed. "I should have called you but it's been hectic here, as you can imagine."

"Stories about it everywhere. You were the one who discovered his body?"

"Unfortunately."

"Throat slit?"

"Yes."

"A razor, they say."

"They're not sure."

"And you're still there."

"Of course I'm still here."

"Don't you think, bein' the smart lady that you are, that it'd be best to scoot right back home here?"

"I considered that, Seth. But Laurie needs me. Needs someone. She's trying to cope with her grief, run the inn, handle calls from the press—she needs my help."

His silence said much.

"Seth, are you there?" I asked.

"Ayah, I'm here. You know, Jessica, I never steered you wrong, did I? Got you through that bad case 'a pneumonia last wintah."

"That's right."

"Well, seems to me you've got yourself smack dab in the middle of a dangerous situation. Got a madman with a razor runnin' about slittin' people's throats. Won't matter to a madman with a razor whether you're a man or woman. Seems to me you *and* Laurie oughta nip off back here."

"I'll be coming home the minute I feel Laurie doesn't need me any longer. Until then—"

"Jessica, you are some jo-jeezly."

"I may be stubborn, Seth, but I am also faithful to my friends. Now stop worrying. What's new in Cabot Cove?"

"Been blessed with a bit of a thaw. Spring's in the air. That's for sure."

"I'm glad. I have an appointment. Got to run. Thanks for calling. Best to everyone."

"Jessica."

"Yes?"

"You take care. Heah?"

"I 'heah' loud-and-clear. Bye, Seth. Miss you."

Having talked to Seth stabbed me with nostalgia. What had been a welcome respite from the cold winter of Maine, from sickness and from a tight deadline, had turned into a grim nightmare. I was aware, of course, that what he *hadn't* said represented a certain truth about me. I was staying at Lover's Lagoon Inn and on St. Thomas not only because I wished to be of help to Laurie, but because I had a need to be involved in sorting out Walter's murder. I hadn't been thrust involuntarily into that role. I could have packed up and left at any time, once questioned by the police. But the desire to help Laurie aside, to walk away without having satisfied my own intellectual curiosity, if nothing else, would be anathema to me. There were questions I wanted answered.

I was a few minutes early for my date with Jennifer Fletcher and used the time to explore other areas of Diamond Reef. It was even larger than I'd realized. There were two Olympic-size pools, one freshwater, one saltwater, tennis courts with lights for night play, shuffleboard, basketball hoops, and bronzed bodies everywhere. Everyone seemed happy and contented; hard to conceive of all the strife that existed between this and Lover's Lagoon Inn. Hard to conceive that less than twenty-four hours ago I'd stepped on Walter Marschalk's very dead hand. The thought sent a chill through me.

I was relieved to see that Jennifer was alone in Room 1202. Her angry friend, Mr. Capehart, was nowhere in sight. Jennifer looked lovely, and perfectly Caribbean in a loose, yellow-and-green sundress, and sandals. "I ordered a pitcher of iced tea and some desserts from room service," she said, pointing to a small balcony reached through a sliding glass door. She led me to it. It overlooked the back of the property where a golf course beckoned.

"Everyone at the conference is in shock about Walter," she said.

"I would imagine," I said. "Such a sick act."

"Do the police have any motives, suspects?"

"Not that I know of. Have you been interviewed yet by the police?"

"I received a call from a Detective Calish. I couldn't imagine why they wanted to talk to me. But then he told me you'd mentioned that we had dinner together last night, and that you'd found the body."

"That's right," I said. "And his name is Calid. Detective Calid."

"Calid, Calish, whatever. He's coming by tonight to interview me. I told him I was busy with the conference but—I guess murder takes precedence."

"It usually does. Let me ask you why, if you're so busy, you wanted to see me?"

"I really don't know," she replied, taking a miniature margarita pie from a tray and popping it into her mouth. She poured two glasses of iced tea and handed one to me. She was overtly nervous and did what nervous people usually do, make an inappropriate gesture. She held up her glass in a misguided toast. I tipped my glass toward her and sipped.

"Have one?" she said, offering me the tray. "The butterscotch brownies are delicious. I've become addicted."

"Thank you, no. It never would have occurred to me to contact you with the intention of asking personal questions. But since you've asked me here, there are a few."

"Personal questions?"

"Yes. I had the distinct feeling at dinner the other night that your friend, Fred, was jealous of you and—well, to be candid, jealous of you and Walter Marschalk."

Her increased nervousness was heralded by a thin, high-pitched, forced laugh. "Jealous of me and Walter?" she said.

"That was my impression."

"Why would he be jealous of Walter? He's—he's dead."

"He wasn't then," I said.

She took a strand of hair she'd been twirling and put it into her mouth, swiveled her head 180 degrees. "A lot of people were jealous of Walter," she said, her gaze directed out over the golf course. "Other travel writers envied him. He was the best-known travel writer in the business. Every one of his books were best-sellers. He wrote for all the major magazines, and the most luxurious hotels around the world wooed him." She now looked at me. "And then he ends up fulfilling every travel writer's dream, to own a beautiful inn on a beautiful island."

That she'd shifted focus from personal jealousy to one of professional envy wasn't lost on me. I patiently heard her out. When she was finished, I asked, "Were any of these envious travel writers jealous enough to want him dead?"

"No."

"How can you be sure?" I asked.

"Just because—Look, Mrs. Fletcher—it sounds funny calling someone else 'Fletcher'—being envious of another writer doesn't usually translate into murder. Forget envy. Lots of people just plain didn't like Walter. He's—he was a very difficult man, cantankerous, pompous, sometimes mean-spirited. We have a writer at the conference who's known Walter for a long time. Larry Lippman. Larry detests Walter and never tries to hide it. But *kill* him? Larry's the sweetest guy in the business, loved by everyone. Don't you have somebody you dislike? Does that mean you'd kill that person?"

"Of course not. What about Fred Capehart?" I asked.

She got up and disappeared into the room. When she returned, I could see that she'd been crying and had wiped her eyes. Smeared makeup said that to me. She sat and said, "I'm ashamed of saying bad things about Walter. He's dead. A lot of the writers have been saying nasty things about him today. They say they're sorry he was killed, but then go right on making sarcastic comments, even sick jokes."

My response was twofold. First, that she was right. It seems to me that when you're dead, all bets should be off, as they say.

Second, what she'd said about Walter's reputation had had a mildly shocking effect upon me. I realized how little I knew about him, his career, his relationships, and his stature within his industry. I had no idea he was the icon she represented him to be. Or that he was disliked by so many colleagues.

"Is there anything else you'd like to ask me?" Jennifer said. Her voice had taken on a surly tone, as though annoyed with my presence. But she'd been the one who'd asked that we meet. Why? The only logical answer was that she wanted to find out what I knew about Walter's murder, and perhaps about the situation at Lover's Lagoon Inn.

I decided to not linger any longer. I asked directly, "Was your friend, Fred Capehart, justified in exhibiting jealousy of you and Walter?"

"If you mean did he know that Walter and I were—"

"Were lovers?"

"Fred is a very jealous person. Of *everyone*. We

used to be boyfriend-girlfriend but it's been over for six months, maybe longer. His jealousy ruined it for us. It's a sickness. He sees men behind every tree."

"Yes, jealousy taken to the extreme is a sickness," I offered.

"It wouldn't be so bad if it really were over. But he's obsessed with me. Like those stalkers you read about, and see on TV. He calls me constantly, and keeps tabs on all my trips. It's easy for him to do that because we're in the same business. Not full-time for him. He shifted into writing about things other than travel. But he still freelances for travel magazines, and receives invitations to a lot of the same press trips. He knows where and when all the big travel conferences are. He knew I was coming to St. Thomas for this one and said he was turning down his invitation. And then he shows up. You know why?"

"Because you were here at a resort next door to the one owned by Walter Marschalk."

"Yes. That's what you wanted to know, isn't it?"

I couldn't help but laugh. "I didn't want to know anything," I said, comfortable with my lie. I had at the top of my "To Do" list to call Jennifer and arrange to get together. She'd beat me to it. A minor point, one not worth bringing up.

She ignored my comment and said, "I was shocked when he showed up here on St. Thomas. The night you and I met—at dinner—he was abusive and rude. I don't have to tell you that. After you left the table, he lashed into me about Walter. He was beside himself. He—"

"Were you and Walter lovers?" I again asked.

"Is that why you came here?" she asked. "To snoop on my private life?"

"You invited me for this little chat, Jennifer."

"You're a very snoopy lady, aren't you, Jessica?"

"Am I curious? Yes. Especially when a very dear friend has had his throat slit."

"*Very dear friend?*" Her expression was as animated as her voice.

"Yes. We were neighbors for years in my hometown in Maine."

"I wish you'd told me that."

"It really shouldn't matter. Walter Marschalk is dead. I'd like to find out why, and who did it."

"Walter and I had an affair." She said it as though she'd just announced that the sun had risen, or that her car needed an oil change.

But then her posture and demeanor changed. She slumped in her chair and tears rolled down her cheeks. She dabbed at them with a hanky, drew deep breaths, and looked directly at me, her eyes searching for some sign that it was okay that she and Walter had been intimate. She didn't need my approval. This wasn't a confessional, at least in any religious sense. What two people decide to do with their lives is their choice, as long as it doesn't hurt, or cost others.

What I didn't express was that I was upset to have learned that Walter had been unfaithful to his wife, Laurie. No morality involved. I'd been his friend. More important, especially since his death, I was the only "old" friend upon which his widow could lean.

Did Laurie Marschalk know about her husband's affair with this attractive younger woman?

109

And the bigger question: Was this an isolated incident, or did it represent a pattern with him?

"Jennifer, how long ago did you and Walter have this affair?"

"Two years ago. It's been—it's been on and off over the years."

"Still going on?" I asked. "Until his death?"

"Not really."

I've always hated the answer, "not really." It screams, at least to me, that there's truth to whatever has been raised. Either something is, or it isn't.

"And Fred knew that you and Walter were still seeing each other?"

"I didn't say that we were."

"I think you did."

"It was more than that."

"Meaning?"

"Meaning—nothing."

"Did you work together?" I asked.

"Why do you ask that? We were in the same business."

I didn't understand her defensiveness but didn't probe. I decided it was time to leave. "I'd best be going," I said, standing. "I know it hasn't been easy talking about your relationship with Walter, nor has it been easy for me to hear."

"Walter's wife is your friend, too?" she asked.

"Yes. I had lunch with her today. Naturally, she's very upset." I thought of the divorce papers and couldn't help but wonder just how upset Laurie really was.

"You won't mention any of this to her."

"Of course not."

"Good, because I wasn't the only one."

"Oh?"

"Walter had plenty of women. Everywhere he went."

"I'm sorry to hear that," I said.

She put on a large red straw hat, picked up her bag, and accompanied me down to the sprawling, rococo lobby that was all glittering gold and red. As we prepared to part at the main entrance—she was on her way to a meeting—she said, "Jessica, there's something else."

"Yes?"

"My jealous friend, Fred Capehart?"

"Yes?"

"He's gone."

"Gone where?"

"I wish I knew. He hasn't shown up at any of the meetings today."

"Have you checked his room?"

"Sure. I checked everywhere. He's disappeared."

"When was the last time you saw him?" I asked.

"Dinner last night. We argued and he left."

"What time was that?"

"About eleven-thirty. He said he needed to think, was going to take a walk. He wanted me to come with him but I was angry. He went alone."

"A walk. Any idea where he walked?"

She paused, looked down at the floor, then up at me. "Lover's Lagoon. He said he was going down to the lagoon."

Chapter 10

A sizable contingent of people with a possible motive for killing Walter Marschalk was suddenly gone. I say "motive" not because they were suspects; that was up to Detective Calid and his St. Thomas police department. But they were "connected" to Walter in ways that too often result in a rationale to murder.

Two people who were involved with Walter in Lover's Lagoon Inn—his partner Chris Webb, and his connection in the St. Thomas Legislature, Bobby Jensen—had left the island. Now, according to Jennifer Fletcher, a young travel writer, Fred Capehart, who evidently harbored a deep dislike for Walter, was nowhere to be found.

Thomas was at the door when I arrived at my villa. "Good afternoon, Mrs. Fletcher," he said.

"Hello, Thomas." I looked past him to the other villas, and beyond to the main house. There wasn't a soul to be seen. "Have *all* the guests checked out?" I asked.

"Yes, ma'am. A new couple checked in today, however. Mr. and Mrs. Sims. Mrs. Marschalk considered closing the inn, but with guests to serve—"

"Yes, I suppose she has an obligation, even to one couple. Not very cost-effective, but necessary."

"Actually, Mrs. Marschalk wanted me to speak with you about something."

"Oh?"

"If you intend to stay, she wonders whether you might be more—more comfortable in the main house. There are rooms there. Empty rooms. I can move your things there now."

I was certain he meant I'd be more *secure.* "No," I said, smiling. "I'm perfectly—comfortable—right here in Villa Number Ten. But thank you for suggesting it."

"As you wish. Would you care for a drink?"

"One of your frosty island concoctions would be nice," I said. "Is Mrs. Marschalk in her office?"

"No, ma'am. She left two hours ago to go into town."

"Shopping?"

"I don't think so. She was taken by the police."

"By the police? Detective Calid?"

"No, ma'am. Uniformed officers. I'll get that drink for you now."

The moment he was gone, I bypassed the inn's switchboard and dialed an outside operator. "St. Thomas police, please. In Charlotte Amalie."

It seemed an eternity before the call went through. "Detective Calid, please."

"Sorry. Detective Calid is not available."

"May I speak then with someone else working on the Marschalk murder?"

"Sorry. No one assigned to that case is available right now. They're all out in the field. May I ask who's calling? I'll leave a message for Detective Calid."

"Yes. Please tell Detective Calid that Jessica Fletcher called."

"Oh, Mrs. Fletcher. I heard you were a guest on the island. My daughter reads your books. She—please hold for Detective Calid."

113

Calid, who must have been sitting next to the officer, came on the line. "Hello, Mrs. Fletcher," he said.

"Hello, Detective. Sorry to bother you. I'm actually calling for two reasons. First, to satisfy my curiosity about how the case is coming along. Second, I understand Mrs. Marschalk is with you."

"To answer your first question, Mrs. Fletcher, things are progressing nicely with the case, thank you." His voice was pleasant, but I detected a hint of annoyance. I wouldn't be deterred by that. After all, I'd been the one to discover the body. That gave me certain rights, I felt, the least of which was the freedom to ask a few questions about the status of the investigation.

"As for your second question," he said, "Mrs. Marschalk left our offices fifteen minutes ago. She's en route to Lover's Lagoon as we speak."

I was relieved. I had visions of the police finding a bloody straight razor in Laurie's purse, and wringing a confession from her that she killed Walter not only because he wouldn't agree to a divorce, but also because he'd been a busy philanderer. I suppose that's the problem with being a writer of fiction, especially on the subject of murder. I never have any problem conjuring scenarios.

"She was escorted home by one of our officers," Calid said.

"Was she with you for further questioning?" I asked.

He chuckled. "Perhaps you'd best ask her about that, Mrs. Fletcher. I will tell you that she will be under twenty-four hour protection for the duration of the investigation."

"You feel she's in danger?" I asked.

"Simply precaution. I was sorry to hear that you'll be leaving us."

"I am?"

"Mrs. Marschalk said that because she's closing Lover's Lagoon, you'd be going home."

"That's news to me," I said. "I haven't been told this, but I'll ask her about that, too."

"Have *you* received any death threats, Mrs. Fletcher?"

"Heavens, no. Why would anyone want to kill me?"

"The same question I had about the Marschalks."

"Marschalks? Both of them?"

"Yes."

"I take it you know about the threatening note Walter received."

"Yes. We found it in his possessions. Frankly, I'm surprised that you knew about it but failed to mention it when we talked."

"It slipped my mind. Mrs. Marschalk has also received one?"

"The reason for providing security for her."

"A prudent decision."

"I thought so."

"Well, thank you for your time," I said. "I'm sure you're very busy."

"Nothing unusual. You know, Mrs. Fletcher, going home might be a prudent decision on *your* part."

"Am I in danger?"

"Of course not. But with the inn closed, it will be lonely for you there."

"I'll give it serious consideration," I said. "Again, thank you."

"My pleasure. And rest assured that should we come up with Mr. Marschalk's murderer, you'll be among the first to know." He laughed. "Enjoy your evening." The sarcasm in his voice was unmistakable, but I forgave him. The last thing he needed was a nosy writer of murder mysteries calling for answers he didn't have.

I dialed Laurie's private office number at the main house and was taken aback when Walter answered—on the answering machine: *"Hello. Sorry Laurie and I can't come to the phone right now, but if you leave a brief message following the tone, we'll be happy to return your call."*

I'd suggest to Laurie that she change the message on the answering machine (had she forgotten to, or did Walter's recorded voice provide comfort?). But I'd wait to tell her in person. The beep sounded and I spoke, albeit uncomfortably. I detest answering machines. "Laurie, it's Jessica. Just calling to see how you were and to suggest we have—" I sensed someone watching me, turned, and saw Thomas standing in the doorway, my drink on a tray. "Just a moment," I said to him, my hand over the mouthpiece. A dial tone pierced my ear. The machine had cut me off. Undoubtedly one of those voice-activated models. Keep talking or your time is up.

I took the drink from Thomas, went to the terrace, sat in a chair, and enjoyed the cold, sweet coconut-flavored liquid in my throat and mouth. I was glad I hadn't been able to complete my message on the machine. I didn't have dinner plans with Laurie, which suited me. I'd decided while talking to Detective Calid that I would take Mark Dobson up on his standing invitation to join the travel writers at Diamond Reef. Somehow, I felt the answers to some of my questions about Walter—and perhaps about his murder—might come from that group.

I dialed the inn's desk. "This is Mrs. Fletcher in Number Ten. Please leave a message for Mrs. Marschalk that I'll be having dinner this evening with friends who arrived unexpectedly on St. Thomas. I'll call her this evening when I return."

I pulled Mark Dobson's card from my purse and called him. "Sorry to hear about your friend's untimely demise," he said, not sounding especially sorry. I'd give him the benefit of the doubt.

"Thank you," I said.

"I understand the inn is closing tomorrow. Will you be leaving along with the other guests?"

Everyone seemed to know Lover's Lagoon Inn was closing except me. But I didn't want to give him the satisfaction of knowing that. "I'm not sure what my plans are at this time," I said. "But I think it might be my final opportunity to take you up on your very generous dinner invitation."

"We'd be honored to have you grace our dining room with your presence." He was smooth. I'd give him that. And crass. He added, "I don't imagine the food's so gourmet these days over there."

"I wouldn't go that far," I said. "Will the travel writers be having dinner together tonight?"

"Absolutely. Tonight is a theme dinner. Reggae night."

Exactly what I wasn't in the mood for. But I'd make a go of it. I didn't want to miss an opportunity to meet with people who had known Walter a lot better than I thought I had.

"Sounds nice," I said. "What time?"

"Cocktails at seven on the patio. Dinner at eight." I checked my watch. Five-thirty. "We all look forward to having you as our guest this evening, Jessica."

I hung up, settled on the terrace, and indulged in the orderly, pleasant task of making notes. As I wrote, my thoughts became clearer and more focused, as usually happens.

Laurie also receives death threat.

I wondered what form it had taken. A written note? Threatening phone call? A crudely drawn symbol representing death?

I allowed my thoughts to roam freely. Laurie receiving a threat was, of course, ominous and cause for concern. On the other hand—and I'm capable of brutal honesty when discussing things with myself—I had to admit (only to me, of course) that my overactive writer's imagination that sprung to life when Laurie was taken to police headquarters was more than fanciful fictitious plotting. Learning that she'd filed for divorce prior to Walter's murder had caused me to wonder whether *she* might have been glad to see him dead. But if she, too, had been threatened, that scenario was unlikely.

Provided threat was legitimate.
Divorce. Who knew?

Had Laurie told anyone else that she was taking action to end her marriage to Walter? Did *their* partner in Lover's Lagoon Inn, Chris Webb, know? Bobby Jensen? The inn's staff?

Jennifer Fletcher?

If Walter knew that his wife was instituting divorce proceedings—and *if* my assumption that the affair between Jennifer and Walter had been ongoing up until the time of his death was correct, he might have told his paramour about this complication in his life. Or lessening of complications, depending upon how he viewed it.

Money.

I'd been thinking all along that if Walter had balked at granting Laurie a divorce, that might have been motive for her to want him dead (forgive me, Laurie, for even thinking such a thing.) In fact, I'd focused almost exclusively on someone having a personal grudge against him.

But money has always ranked high on the motive-for-murder list, certainly as high as such staples as jealousy and envy, pride, anger, and blackmail. Greed twists people every day into irrational states. And what is more irrational than murder?

I'd observed that Walter and Chris Webb did not have what might be termed a copacetic business partnership. There was tension there. And I was aware that money pressures on Walter and Laurie were considerable. Had they bribed Bobby Jensen in order to buy Lover's Lagoon Inn? If so, had Jensen become dissatisfied with the financial arrangement and pushed for a bigger payoff? Possible.

Jealousy?

Jennifer didn't strike me as the sort of woman who would put undue pressure on a married man to leave his wife. But I hardly knew her. If Walter had promised to leave Laurie for Jennifer, but reneged on the promise, it could result in a very angry young woman. Angry enough to kill? Not likely. But it wouldn't be the first time. And how ironic if Walter had decided to stay with Laurie, not knowing *she* was about to end the marriage, but Jennifer didn't know?

So many suppositions, questions, what-ifs, and whys.

A couple sauntered in the direction of the lagoon. I assumed they were the new guests, the Simses, that Thomas had mentioned. The man was considerably older than the woman; at least twenty years in my judgment. He struck me as the sort of man who didn't like growing older. Thinning gray hair had been combed up from just above his right ear and up over his bald pate. He walked with a swagger, as though it took effort to keep his stomach sucked in. She was trim, deeply tanned, and had silver-blond hair. She wore a tiny white bikini. He was dressed in red bathing trunks and a flowered shirt. A point-and-shoot camera on a strap dangled from his neck.

Were they aware that a murder had taken place on the now pristine white sand of the lagoon? Maybe that was why they were going down there, to see the murder scene, photograph it, add it to their St. Thomas vacation photo album.

They passed from my view, then reemerged in the water where they embraced and kissed. Don't be so cynical, Jess, I told myself as I went inside to dress for dinner. Walter Marschalk's murder wasn't consuming everyone's hearts and minds.

I washed my face and applied makeup carefully, something I hadn't done since arriving at the inn. I put on a gold, raw silk pantsuit to which I'd treated myself on a winter shopping excursion to Bangor in anticipation of trading in Maine's long, bone-chilling winter for balmy, Caribbean evenings sipping piña coladas beneath the palms. I studied myself in the full-length mirror. I like the way I looked in the pantsuit. Its cut was flattering, and the heat of the day had naturally shaped my hair in a pleasing way that I never could have achieved myself.

Had Walter looked in the mirror yesterday morning and felt good about the way he looked?

Our fragile, tenuous hold on life was very much on my mind as I left the villa and headed for Diamond Reef.

Chapter 11

The first familiar face I spotted on the patio at Diamond Reef was Jennifer Fletcher. She wore a striking white dress that hugged her thighs, and a narrow-brimmed white straw hat. Her tan had deepened over the past few hours to the shade of coffee dark, no sugar. Maybe it was an illusion brought about by the stark contrast of copper skin against white clothing. Or the application of one of those fake tan creams. Whatever the reason, she was stunning, a perfect model for a Caribbean travel ad.

She was flanked by two men—an older man who looked to me like a stand-in for Detective Colombo of TV fame, and a much younger man with hair bleached blond by the sun, aided and abetted perhaps by a drugstore concoction. Each held an exotic tropical drink in a tall glass topped with fruit and a tiny umbrella. Did the drinks glow in the dark? I wondered. They were enjoying a good laugh when Jennifer spotted me and headed my way.

"You look lovely," I said.

"So do you," she replied. "I'm so glad you'll be having dinner with us. Everyone is excited." She leaned closer and whispered over the rolling sound of a steel drum band, "Mark Dobson called each of us in our rooms to tell us you'd be joining us."

"How embarrassing," I said.

She whispered again. "By the way, Jessica, my

friend, Fred, has resurfaced. He called me a little while ago."

"Where was he?"

"He wouldn't tell me, but it was long-distance. I know that."

I was about to ask another question about Fred Capehart's whereabouts when the resort's general manager, Mark Dobson, joined us. "Hello, Jessica," he said, extending his hand. "I can't tell you how pleased I am to be your host this evening. A drink? We're all enjoying a Lover's Lagoon. It's made with dark and light rums, coconut milk, pineapple, and kahlua." He smiled broadly.

I'd already learned from Thomas what was in a Lover's Lagoon cocktail. My prior knowledge aside, the lack of good taste in offering me a Lover's Lagoon cocktail on the heels of Walter's brutal murder was enough reason to turn down his offer. I expected him to add "blood" to the list of ingredients. "White wine would be fine," I said.

"White wine it is." He waved for a half-naked waitress to take my order, grasped my elbow with one hand, and with his other hand steadying his crutch led me in the direction of a knot of people I assumed were the travel writers.

"Can I have everyone's attention please," he announced. "Allow me to introduce Diamond Reef's very special guest for dinner this evening, the world's most renowned writer of murder mysteries, Jessica Fletcher."

I was reticent as I stepped forward to shake each person's hand. Dobson's introduction had been unnecessarily rococo. I've always been uncomfortable in such situations, although years of dealing with it have developed a certain ability to cope. I wished Dobson had simply introduced me by name and let it go at that. But he hadn't, and I pressed the flesh as politicians are skilled at doing, grateful when my wine arrived to provide a different focus.

The only person whose name was familiar was Larry Lippman, whom Jennifer had mentioned earlier that day. He may have disliked Walter Marschalk, but his kindly face and self-effacing demeanor told me he was no killer. Still, I'd make it a point to speak with him before the evening was over. He must have disliked Walter for a reason, and I wanted to know what that reason was, what *all* the reasons were for harboring ill-feelings for my murdered host.

I thought the introduction "ceremony" was over. But after I'd been introduced to the last person in the group, Dobson said, "Let's all give Jessica Fletcher a warm Diamond Reef welcome."

This can't be happening, I thought, as they applauded.

Jennifer said into my ear, "Jessica, I'd like to introduce you to a few special friends of mine." She pointed to the two men with whom she'd been talking when I arrived. The minute we walked away from the larger group she said, chuckling, "I saved you. Mark can be so over-bearing at times."

"This was certainly one of them," I said.

"Stick with me," Jennifer said. "I know the clowns to stay away from and the ones who are okay. I'll make sure you have a good time."

Somehow, I had the feeling Jennifer always saw

to it that she, and whomever she was with had a good time. Maybe to a fault.

The Colombo look-alike's name was Joe Spinosa. He stood out from everyone else at Diamond Reef the way a woman in a bikini would stand out at a Wall Street board meeting. He wore a rumpled greenish suit, white shirt with ring-around-the-collar and with collar points that curled up like flowers seeking water, a skinny black tie, and heavy black shoes. He needed a shave; his hair needed washing. Other than that, he had a craggy, infectious smile and quick wit.

The younger blond man, who wore red-and-white swim trunks, rubber thongs, and a white T-shirt with a slightly risqué message, was Zachary Alexander. "Zach does the Caribbean section for some of the top guidebooks," Jennifer said.

"Top guidebooks, but not top pay," he said without any inflection of dissatisfaction. He laughed, in fact. Alexander and Spinosa were extreme opposites, but shared a likability. I silently hoped I'd get to sit near them at dinner, especially Spinosa, who made me laugh with caustic comments that slid out of the side of his mouth—where a cigar should be.

As it turned out, Jennifer sat to my right, Spinosa to my left, with Lippman directly across from me. Mark Dobson was at the head of the table, not only because he was the dinner's host, but because he needed room for his cast, which he propped on an empty chair.

After we'd taken our seats in what was billed as an "authentic British pub"—one of Diamond Reef's seven restaurants—Jennifer leaned close and said, "Joe and I rearranged the seating chart so we could sit next to you. Hope you don't mind.

Believe me, you're better off. The writer Dobson had next to you is weird. A real space cadet. She hasn't even shown up tonight. Sometimes she shows up for things, sometimes she doesn't."

I had trouble hearing Jennifer because the soft, lilting strains of the steel drum band on the terrace had been replaced by the pub's stereo system, whose volume control had evidently been altered to exclude all but its highest setting. Fortunately, the waiter complained he couldn't take our orders because he couldn't hear over the music. Dobson instructed the bartender to turn it down. The relative silence was blissful.

We ordered from a strangely eclectic menu— British pub fare such as kidney pie or cottage pie, a baked mix of ground beef topped with mashed potato—and Caribbean dishes, most featuring conch served as fritters, chowder, salad, or standalone (conch) with various sauces. I yearned for something out of Laurie Marschalk's kitchen. Would she ever cook again at Lover's Lagoon Inn? She'd have to prepare some semblance of meals for her two guests, the Simses. And for me, although I wouldn't expect her to create meals on my account. What a mess, I thought as my attention returned to Mark Dobson, who held court at the table, a large mug of ale in his hand. He was in the middle of a long tale about Diamond Reef having hosted a "Born Again and Loving It" convention when the waiter brought him a cordless phone.

"Not now," Dobson said.

"It's Senator Jensen. Long distance. He says it's important."

I cocked an ear in Dobson's direction. He surveyed the table, handed the phone back to the

126

waiter, struggled to his feet, and said, "I'll take it in my office."

I watched him move across the pub and out the door. Why would *he* be receiving a long distance call from island Senator Bobby Jensen? Jensen supposedly was a close friend of Laurie and Walter. I could understand a call from another senator, the one Jensen told me was on Diamond Reef's payroll and who'd initiated the investigation into the purchase of Lover's Lagoon by the Marschalks.

I didn't have time to ponder it because Joe Spinosa said loudly to the table, "Maybe Walter Marschalk will attend next year's Born Again and Loving It convention."

I winced. Everyone, except Jennifer, broke into raucous laughter. "Sorry," she whispered to me. I shrugged. Spinosa didn't know of my relationship with the Marschalks, probably never even realized I would know the name. His comment generated a succession of nasty comments about Walter, each intended to be funny. And then individuals started telling "Walter stories," few of which were flattering. If I'd decided to attend the dinner in the hope of gaining insight into why Walter was disliked by his professional colleagues, I'd made the right decision. Although these specific words weren't used, I got the impression that Walter was considered by the people at the table to be egotistical, greedy, cruel, dishonest, insensitive, conniving, paranoid, schizophrenic, lustful, and foul. The only redeeming value mentioned was "boring."

Hardly the Walter Marschalk I'd known and loved back in Cabot Cove. If there was even a modicum of truth to what they said about him,

127

Laurie hadn't been nearly as astute in choosing him as a mate as when choosing ingredients for her gourmet dishes.

Lippman said, "I'll tell you one thing about Marschalk. He sure as hell knew how to run an inn."

"Bull," another writer said. "His *wife* knows how to run an inn."

"That's right," someone else chimed in. "The only thing Walter knew was how to steal the money to buy it."

"So what?" Spinosa said. "That's important. Getting the money. I mean, hell, that's all a Broadway or Hollywood producer does, get the money. Without it, you got bubkes." His words were slurred; too much rum will do it every time.

A middle-aged woman said, "That inn of Walter's is gorgeous. I haven't been in the rooms, but—well, Jennifer can probably tell you about them."

"Especially the beds," Spinosa said.

More loud laughter. Jennifer's affair with Walter was obviously public knowledge, at least with this group. She tossed a visual dagger at Spinosa, excused herself, and headed for the rest rooms.

"Geez, I'm in trouble now," Spinosa said. He started to follow her but I put my hand on his arm. "She'll be fine," I said. "I'll check on her if she isn't back in a few minutes."

He grinned. "Guess I couldn't follow her in where she's going anyway," he said.

Lippman said from across the table, "I love your books, Mrs. Fletcher. Got any new ones coming out?"

"As a matter of fact, I just finished my latest

before coming to St. Thomas. Sort of a reward for myself."

"How long does it take you to write a book?" he asked.

"Depends. If the plot is worked out, it goes rather quickly."

"Is that the toughest part? Coming up with a plot?"

"Usually."

"You could do your next novel based on what happened next door," Spinosa said. "Wouldn't have to make up anything."

I gave him my best quizzical look.

"Maybe you don't know about the murder."

"Oh, I certainly heard about it," I said. "Walter Marschalk is the one you've been talking about."

"That's right," said Lippman.

"Not an especially popular fellow, I take it."

There was laughter around the table. "An understatement, Mrs. Fletcher," Spinosa said.

"Someone as unpopular as this Marschalk must have had many enemies," I said.

"As many enemies as people he met," a woman said.

"That's quite a condemnation," I said.

"Am I wrong?" she asked her colleagues, none of whom demurred.

"What was it about him that—?"

My question was interrupted by Mark Dobson's return. His face lacked its earlier sparkle. In fact, he looked downright distraught. But after settling in his place, leg resting on the empty chair beside him, he smiled broadly. "Everyone having a good time?" he asked.

"Terrific," Lippman replied.

"I couldn't help but overhear that you got a call from—" I started to say to Dobson but, as if on cue, Jennifer came back to the table. Joe Spinosa put his arm around her and whispered in her ear, an apology I assumed for his ill-considered remark. I examined her pretty face. She'd obviously been crying but had sufficiently pulled herself together to announce with a smile, "Sorry, gang, but I have to run." She waved off protests and said, "Catch you all at breakfast. 'Bye!"

"Sorry you have to leave," I said when she came around the table to personally bid me good night.

"Me, too, Mrs. Fletcher. I'm not feeling well. I think I need an early-to-bed night."

"Please. Make it Jessica. Sounds appealing. An early-to-bed night."

"Jessica." Her smile was wan. "Maybe we'll get a chance to talk again—just the two of us."

"Let's make a point of it," I said. "Good night."

I wanted to go with her as much as I wanted to ask Mark Dobson about his call from Senator Bobby Jensen. But Jennifer hadn't invited me, and I didn't want to be too blatant in asking Dobson about the call. Dinner was served, and the conversation was dominated by tales of the travel writer's life. Everyone at the table was a fountain of stories, many of them insider yarns that kept the laughter going, fueled by the uninterrupted flow of rum drinks. I tried on a few occasions to slip in questions about Walter Marschalk, but they got lost in the barrage of jokes and confessions.

I eventually decided to sit back and enjoy the banter, take it all in. I sat quietly and ate my dinner, laughed a lot, answered the few questions asked of me about my writing career and habits, and went with the flow, as they say.

Actually, I enjoyed myself more than I thought I would. A stilted crowd this was not. A spirited argument broke out on the merits of a recent movie everyone had seen except me, and then about a *New York Times* article on the subject of traveling alone that I had read just days before leaving for St. Thomas.

"It was a dumb article," Lippman said. "Bring a book to dinner with you," he said in a whiny, exaggerated voice. "I mean, come on. You don't have to be a rocket scientist to figure that out. If you need to get that piece of advice from an article in the *Times,* you deserve to travel alone."

There was a momentary lull as dessert was served. "It sounds like such an exciting life," I said, "the life of a travel writer. Do you all enjoy it as much as you seem to?"

Lippman smiled, looked at his colleagues, laughed loudly, and said, "Yeah, it's fun, but it can be grueling. The constant travel can be hard on a family, which takes its toll on you."

A man, whose nickname was Sully, added, "I've been home one weekend all month. I'll get to take my wife *and* kids with me next week to Jamaica."

"You're bringing your kids to Jamaica?" Spinosa said. "Think I'll cancel my plans."

"It's a single person's game," Zachary Alexander said. He'd had little to say all evening, his attention focused on a pretty young woman who, I recalled, worked for a travel newsletter.

"Yes, I can see how it would be," I said.

"Ask Marschalk," a woman said.

The mention of his name brought forth a fresh round of comments about Walter, including tasteless jokes, a few of them provided by Mark Dobson. I decided I'd had enough. "This was a wonderful evening," I said. "Thank you for allowing me to join you."

"Hey, the night's still young, Mrs. Fletcher," said Spinosa.

"But I'm not," I said. I stood and extended my hand to Dobson. "No need to get up, not with that cast," I said.

"I insist," he said. "Back in a few minutes," he said to the group. He waved for the waiter to take a new round of drink orders, and walked me to the main lobby. "Hope they weren't too raucous," he said.

"No, not at all. I enjoyed myself."

"I understand things are pretty bad next door. She's closing the inn."

"I don't think so. New guests checked in only this morning."

His smirk was annoying. "There's a suite reserved for you any time you want it," he said.

"I appreciate that, Mark, but I won't be needing it. Thank you again for a lovely evening."

I was about to leave Diamond Reef but remembered that the tube of toothpaste I'd brought with me to St. Thomas had only one final squeeze left in it. A notions shop off the lobby was still open. I went into it, purchased a new tube at a price that would have bought four tubes back home, perused the magazines, newspapers, and paperback books (two copies of mine were there), and walked across the lobby toward the main entrance. I reached the door, started to open it, stopped, and stepped back behind potted foliage.

I parted fronds in the best tradition of a hotel detective and narrowed my eyes. What I thought I'd seen was accurate. Jennifer Fletcher was getting into the passenger seat of a long black Mercedes parked at the curb. The man who'd held the door open for her now came around the front of the vehicle, paused, looked left and right, then got behind the wheel, closed his door, and started the engine. It was Chris Webb, the Marschalk's partner in Lover's Lagoon Inn.

I didn't hesitate. The moment the Mercedes had pulled away, I walked quickly to a waiting taxi, got in, and said, "Follow that car."

Chapter 12

"Could you go a little faster?" I asked my driver, an older black man wearing a Chicago Cubs baseball cap backward, who sang along with calypso music that oozed from his radio. A dozen furry little figures dangling from the visors bobbed to the rhythms.

"No good to rush, ma'am," he said, his head moving up and down as though conducting the furry dancers. "Not good for the blood pressure."

"But I don't want to lose that car," I said. The Mercedes was leaving us in the dust, figuratively and literally.

"Not likely we'd lose him, ma'am," he said. "He's heading for Charlotte Amalie, that's for certain. He can't drive very fast over the mountains."

I continued to lean on the back of his seat and attempted to catch a glimpse of Webb's taillights. They came and went, suddenly flashing as red beacons at the top of a hill, then disappearing over the crest. Eventually, they were not to be seen again, and my heart pounded with frustration. But then, after coming down a final twisting, narrow mountain road, I saw the black Mercedes as it slowed to enter the crowded streets of Charlotte Amalie. My driver turned and grinned. "See, ma'am? Not to worry."

Webb maneuvered the Mercedes onto Norre Gade, otherwise known as Main Street, and parked in front of a church. I instructed my driver to also park, leaving plenty of distance between us and the Mercedes. I watched as Jennifer stepped from the passenger side, stretched, yawned, and waited for Webb to join her. When he got out, he slowly walked around the car to ascertain whether he'd parked too far out into the street. He had, but evidently didn't care.

"What is that church?" I asked my driver.

"Frederick Lutheran, ma'am. Second oldest Lutheran church in Western Hemisphere."

"And that building?" I asked, pointing across the street at a building to which Webb and Jennifer were headed.

"Fort Christian. Our oldest building. Completed in 1687. A United States landmark, ma'am. Was once a jail, among other things. Our history museum is located in its dungeons."

"Oh." I felt a chill in the heavy, warm night air as I envisioned the dungeons, sans museum— dark and dank, with chains on the walls and the blood of prisoners on the dirt floors. I've never been fond of jails, and avoid them at all costs, although I've found myself visiting enough of them over the years.

Jennifer and Chris Webb paused in front of the old fort, glanced about, then disappeared around the side of the building.

"Is the museum open this late at night?" I asked my driver.

"Oh, no, ma'am. Closes each day at four-thirty, except for Saturday and Sunday when it closes at four."

I couldn't help but smile. He was a living, breathing St. Thomas guidebook. If I decided to take another tour of the island, I'd make a point of looking him up.

"Where to now, ma'am?"

"I'm—not quite sure. Can we just sit here for a few minutes? With the meter running, of course."

"As you wish." He increased the volume on the radio slightly, turned his hat around and pulled the bill down over his eyes, leaned back and hummed softly along with the music while I sat back to contemplate my next move.

My choices were simple. Sit there and see what happens next, which was likely to be the return of Jennifer and Webb to the Mercedes. Or, get out, follow their path, and see what I could see. The latter course of action made the most sense, at least from the standpoint of accomplishing something. Sitting in a darkened taxi listening to island music, as infectious as it might be, was destined to accomplish nothing except a lofty figure on the meter. On the other hand, following them carried with it certifiable risk. I had no idea where they'd gone after having rounded the corner of the building. For all I knew, they were standing just out of sight. "Hi," I pictured myself saying. "What a coincidence seeing you here in the dark."

"I'll be right back," I said.

The driver sat up and turned to me. "You're taking a walk?" he asked.

"In a manner of speaking," I replied, sliding across the seat and opening the door. "You'll wait?"

"For as long as you wish." We both looked at the meter, its silent, glowing green digital readout keeping tabs of how long we'd been together.

"Careful, ma'am." he said.

I paused halfway out the door. "Of what?" I asked.

136

"Not the safest thing to be doing, a woman alone downtown at night."

"But this is Main Street," I said, observing a number of people walking. "But yes, I'll be careful."

I slowly walked along the sidewalk in front of the church until reaching a point where I could see the side of the fort where Jennifer and Webb had gone. When I did, I slowed to almost a complete stop and narrowed my eyes. All was dark. I saw no one.

But then a flash of light appeared in a window of a small, one-story building in an alley that ran alongside the fort. The light was gone as quickly as it had appeared. Someone had pulled a curtain across the window.

I looked back at the taxi. A single, low-wattage street lamp cast just enough light through the windshield for me to see my driver sitting up straight and looking in my direction. That was comforting. At least someone knew where I was. If something untoward were to happen, he could come to my rescue. If he was so inclined, and it was between songs.

I crossed the street and paused in front of the fort. A car passed, too fast for the narrow street, its driver leaning on his horn to warn pedestrians crossing to get out of his way. A disheveled young man approached and held out three wristwatches he held in his hand. "Cheap," he said. "Thank you, no," I said. For a moment, I thought he would become aggressive but he didn't, just shuffled away in search of another buyer.

It seemed to have become degrees hotter, and the air took on weight; I had trouble breathing. I walked slowly toward the building in which I'd seen light before curtains blotted it out. It was one-story and small, no more than twelve-by-twelve. Peeling green shutters framed the only window. The door was also green, and short. Anyone over six feet would have to stoop to pass through.

Time for another decision. I'd come this far. Should I knock? That was out of the question. If Jennifer Fletcher and Chris Webb were inside—and it was only an assumption on my part—they would be annoyed, at best, at my deliberate intrusion. If they were behind that short green door, it wasn't for the purpose of a party. People don't meet behind closed doors in a dark alley unless there's a reason for secrecy. At least they don't in my books.

As I came closer to the door, gravel crunched beneath my feet, the sound magnified by the stillness of the night. I was only a few feet from the door. I heard voices. The man's was low and unidentified. The woman's voice belonged to Jennifer. I was certain of that.

I stepped right up to the door and pressed my ear to it. The voices were more distinct now. Jennifer said, "He thought he could get away with it." The man, who I was now certain was Webb, although I hadn't heard enough of his voice to make a positive ID, said, "What goes around comes around."

I strained to hear more. The sound of an automobile came from the street, but I paid little attention. Had it passed, or had it stopped?

"Who could blame him?" Jennifer asked.

"Sure—" Webb's words faded.

Who were they talking about? I wondered.

Someone coughed. Webb? No. It came from—

I looked in the direction of the street. A man had turned into the alley and was approaching. He stopped to light a cigarette, which gave me time to step back into the shadows behind a gnarled tree. Cigarette lighted, the man continued toward the small building. I could now see that he wore a pale blue seersucker suit, white shirt, and muted tie. He knocked twice. The door opened, and Jennifer Fletcher greeted him. He tossed his cigarette on to the ground, said "Hi," and stepped inside. The door closed behind him.

Now there were three people inside.

The Marschalks' partner, Chris Webb.

Travel writer and my namesake, Jennifer Fletcher.

And Jennifer's brooding, ardent suitor, Fred Capehart.

Chapter 13

My friends back in Cabot Cove sometimes joke about my ability to sleep no matter what chaos erupts about me. Some would say it represents a clear conscience, although I doubt that my conscience is any clearer than most people's. Whatever the reason, it's always been a blessing. I don't function well without adequate sleep, at least not when faced with writing. Routine chores yes, those things we do by rote. But not where thought is demanded.

And so not being able to sleep after returning from my expensive surveillance trip to Charlotte Amalie only compounded my confusion when the phone rang in my villa at six-thirty the next morning. I'd fallen asleep about four; there was still a few hours of dreams due me.

It was turning into the most exhausting vacation of my life.

"Hello," I mumbled, sounding angry and annoyed. I wasn't either of those things. I may not function well without sleep, but I'm never nasty because of it. I simply could not get my mouth to work the way it usually does.

"Good morning, Mrs. Fletcher." Detective Calid sounded spry and alert. As though he'd had nine hours of blissful sleep. "Did I wake you?"

"No." I sat up against the headboard and tried to force myself awake, to sound as though I'd been up for hours and had already accomplished a day's work. I failed. Another lost Oscar nomination.

If he thought he'd awakened me, he didn't dwell upon the notion. He said cheerily, "I told you you'd be one of the first to know if there was a break in the Marschalk murder case. I wouldn't want to renege on my promise."

Okay, I thought. You've got my attention. The cobwebs are gone, and my eyes are wide-open.

"We've arrested a suspect."

Who needs sleep? I reached for pen and paper I keep on my nighttable. "I'm listening," I said.

"His name is Jacob Austin. He worked at Lover's Lagoon. Walter Marschalk fired him the day before he was killed."

The young man I'd heard arguing with Walter my first morning in the villa, the same one I'd seen while walking with Walter after dinner that night.

"Has he confessed?" I asked.

"Not yet, but we're close to getting one out of him. Actually, we don't need it. We have sufficient evidence."

"Evidence?"

"Yes. To begin with, motive. He'd been fired by Marschalk. Besides, he was known to express his hatred for your friend to anyone who would listen."

"Just motive?"

"Weapon. He'd purchased a straight razor two days before the murder."

"It was the one used to"—I couldn't bring myself to say slash Walter's throat—"to kill Walter?"

"We believe so."

"Was there blood on it? Walter Marschalk's blood?"

The detective laughed, said, "Slow down, Mrs. Fletcher. I've already told you more than I intended. I just thought you'd want to know that it looks like this case will be resolved faster than anticipated."

I wasn't sure how to respond. The young gardener was a likely suspect considering the confrontation he'd had with Walter over being dismissed. As I listened to the detective speak, I could hear Jacob's words to Walter just outside my villa that morning—"*You'll be sorry's all I can say.*"

"I appreciate your call, Detective Calid. Where is this Jacob Austin being held?"

"Our jail in Charlotte Amalie. He was arraigned late last night. No bail. He won't be going anywhere."

I hesitated, then asked, "Would you object to my visiting him?"

"For what purpose, Mrs. Fletcher?"

I knew he would ask why I wanted to visit the accused in jail, and had at-the-ready an answer I've used before when making such a request. "Research for my next book. I've never visited a Caribbean jail before."

"You can accomplish that without seeing the accused," he said. "I'll be happy to take you on a personal tour."

Time for Reason Number Two. "I would like to speak with him for Mrs. Marschalk's sake. It would comfort her if he would tell me, in personal terms, about having murdered her husband."

"Perhaps she'd like to hear that with her own

ears," Calid said. His joviality had vanished. He sounded impatient.

"Does Mrs. Marschalk know this young man has been arrested?" I asked.

"Yes. I phoned her just before calling you."

"Was this Jacob Austin the one who'd sent her a threatening note?"

"He won't admit to that, but we're confident he wrote the note."

"She must be relieved," I said. "Mrs. Marschalk."

"Extremely."

"Well?"

"Well what, Mrs. Fletcher?"

"May I visit the accused?"

"If his attorney agrees, I suppose there's no reason not to grant you that request."

"Who is his attorney?"

"Luther Z. Jackson."

"He has offices in town?"

"Public defender's office." He gave me the number.

"Thank you for the courtesy of your call," I said. "It was thoughtful of you."

I hung up and stretched out on my bed. It was tempting to fall back to sleep, but I forced myself to get up, splash cold water on my face and wrists, and take to the terrace with my notebook. I scribbled some notes but my mind wandered. I checked my watch. It was probably too early to call this attorney, Luther Z. Jackson. Then again, he wasn't in private practice. As a public defender, he undoubtedly spent many nights up and working.

I paced the terrace, thoughts coming and going like zaps of electrical current. "Patience is a virtue," my mother often told me, a philosophy I've always had trouble embracing.

But then a favorite saying of my father came to mind. "Always go with your instincts, Jessica," he would say. I liked that advice a lot better than having to exhibit patience.

I dialed the number given me by Detective Calid. "Luther Z. Jackson," a man answered.

"I'm so glad you're there," I said. "My name is Jessica Fletcher."

For years I've enjoyed trying to match physical appearance with voices heard on the radio, or during a telephone conversation. I'm invariably wrong. Someone who sounds on the air like a big person always turns out to be short and skinny. Blondes prove to be brunets. Baldness usually ends up a full head of hair.

It was no different with attorney Luther Z. Jackson. I had him pegged as a tall, slender man with a long, angular face, rimless glasses, and a slash for a mouth. Instead, he could have been the brother of portly New York TV weatherman Al Roker, my favorite of all television weather pundits. I told Mr. Jackson that he looked like Al Roker.

"I'm mistaken for him all the time when I go back to New York," he said pleasantly as we introduced ourselves to each other in front of the jailhouse. "I have family there. Some days when I'm back there, I get asked more about the weather than about law."

"How are you at weather forecasting?" I asked.

"Better than Al Roker," he replied, "although I suppose there are days he knows more about the law than I do. Come in, Mrs. Fletcher. My client is waiting."

The St. Thomas jail was a long, rectangular building that might have been a military barracks at one time. I imagined its original color to have been pea soup green, or gray; it was now seashell pink, with a gleaming white tile roof. Large baskets of island flowers lined the few steps leading up to the door. Jackson opened it for me, and I stepped into a reception area that shared the same look and feel as the St. Thomas airport. The only difference was the music. Instead of calypso or steel drums, it was the sort of music you hear in elevators in Manhattan, or supermarket aisles in Cabot Cove.

A young woman in uniform sat behind a highly polished desk that contained nothing, not a scrap of paper, pencil, telephone, or calendar. Jackson stepped up to the desk and told her she looked especially lovely this morning. She beamed, said she wished she could say the same about him. They laughed in concert. He was obviously a frequent visitor to the jail, as one would expect of a public defender.

"This is Jessica Fletcher," he said, motioning for me to come to his side. "She's a writer of mystery books, and quite famous."

"You're too kind," I said, accepting the female officer's outstretched hand.

"She's here to spend a little time with my client, Mr. Austin."

"I see." The officer pulled a logbook from beneath the desk and asked me to sign it.

"How is he?" Jackson asked.

"Upset. The night officer says he didn't sleep

145

a wink. Just pacing and shouting that he's inno-cent."

"Which he is," said Jackson.

"And you're paid to say that," the woman retorted.

"Right you are," Jackson said, "but not enough to ask you on a proper date."

"It's nothing to do with money," she said, standing and leading us to a door marked "OFFICIAL PERSONNEL ONLY." "It's your wife who might be a problem."

Jackson looked at me, grinned, and shrugged. "Sometimes I forget about her," he said as the door was opened and we stepped into a corridor lined with individual cells. The first few were empty. If they were any barometer, the crime rate on St. Thomas was low.

But then we passed cells that housed prisoners. Some sat sullenly on their bunks, their eyes silently watching as we passed. One inmate came to the bars, grasped them, and shouted sexual obscenities at me. Jackson took my arm and spir-ited me past that cell as quickly as possible.

Jacob Austin was in a cell at the far end of the corridor. He appeared to be asleep. Jackson said loudly, "Wake up, Jacob."

The young prisoner opened one eye, then the other, but never moved his head.

"Mrs. Fletcher is here. The lady I told you was coming."

"Go away," Austin said.

"Not on your life," said Jackson. "You're in enough trouble without insulting a famous writer who's come here to help you."

Austin pushed up on his elbows and looked at

me. "Hello, Jacob," I said. "I remember you from the inn."

He swung his legs off the cot, stood, stretched, and slowly approached the bars. "Help me?" he said. "You and Marschalk were good friends. Why would you want to help me?"

"Because—" I wasn't prepared for what the attorney had said about my being there to help. I hadn't told him that, nor was I sure it represented what I truly felt. But I suddenly was consumed with exactly that—a belief that this young man had not murdered Walter Marschalk. Don't ask me why, at least not at that juncture. But that's how I felt. I said, "I don't believe you killed my friend, Walter Marschalk."

"You don't?"

"No."

"Why?"

I'd hoped he wouldn't ask that question. But now that he had, I said, "Because you don't appear to me to be the sort of person who would kill anyone. Am I right?"

Jacob didn't respond. The uniformed female officer, who stood slightly behind us, asked, "Going in?"

"Jacob?" Jackson said.

"All right."

We entered the small cell. "Sit on the bed," Austin said. He took a spindly, wobbly chair and sat backwards on it, his arms resting on its back. The officer left, locked us in the cell, and disappeared up the hallway.

"Thank you for seeing me," I said.

He said nothing.

"Jacob, I'd like to hear your side of the story. I'm not with the police, so you don't have to worry about what you say to me." I looked to Jackson to confirm that to his client, which he did by a solemn nod of the head, adding, "They've only granted us twenty minutes, Jacob. I suggest you make the most of it."

Then, something unexpected happened. This surly, noncommunicative, seemingly hardened young man who'd threatened his employer, and who'd been charged with the brutal murder of that employer, began to cry. Tears ran freely down his cheeks. His chest heaved, and he pressed his lips together in an attempt to regain control. Was it jail and its unique ability to soften some men that had brought about this display of human vulnerability? Or was it a window into what Jacob Austin was really like? I didn't ponder the answer, simply handed him a Kleenex from my purse, which he used to dry his eyes and to blow his nose.

"Jacob, I understand if you don't want to talk. But if you do, I'm all ears. As your attorney said, we don't have much time."

Jacob looked at me, his face still wet, his bottom lip trembling. "I didn't do it," he said. "I didn't do anything."

"I heard you threaten Mr. Marschalk," I said. "The morning he fired you."

"I shouldn't have said it. He took the comment as an affirmation of my status as his enemy. But that doesn't mean—"

He cut me off. No more crying. He sat up straight. His mouth and eyes returned to their prior defiant state. "So what if I threatened him?" he said. "I hated him, but so does everybody else who works for him. Maybe I shouldn't have said it, but I did. But I didn't kill him. I swear it."

"Give me a chance to believe you Jacob. I want to believe you."

"I don't know what else to say except that I wasn't even near the inn or Lover's Lagoon that night. I was taking care of my baby. She had a hundred-and-four fever. An ear infection in both ears. She gets them a lot."

"Was there anyone else with you?"

"Sure. My wife and two other kids. I told the cops my wife was there with me but they said she couldn't be an alibi. Because she was my wife. They didn't even question her."

"So there was no one else with you besides your wife and children. How old are they?"

"My wife is—"

"Your children."

"Five, three, and one."

"Too young to be witnesses," said Jackson.

"Jacob, Detective Calid mentioned a straight razor he says you purchased a few days before Mr. Marschalk was killed."

"That's right. A gift for my grandfather. He's old-fashioned, likes to shave with it."

"You gave it to your grandfather?"

"No. I mean, I got it to give to him but I lost it the day I bought it."

"Lost it?"

"Disappeared. I think it might have fallen out of my pocket when I was at work."

"At the inn?"

"Yes. I forgot to leave it home and had it in my jacket along with a lot of other stuff. I lost something else, too, a key chain."

I turned to Jackson, who'd been listening intently. "If the police didn't find the razor," I

149

said, "why would they consider it the murder weapon?"

"They're making assumptions, all circumstantial, Mrs. Fletcher. They found out Jacob bought the razor, got the record of the sale from the shopkeeper, and decided that was sufficient to use as evidence."

"Surely you could have that thrown out of court," I said.

"Depends upon the judge, Mrs. Fletcher. Nothing's for sure in a court."

I returned my attention to Jacob. "Do you know who might have killed Walter Marschalk?" I asked.

"Plenty of people. Like I said, he was hated by just about everybody. And his business was being investigated. The whole island knows that. It was on the front page of the newspaper, for God's sake. It could have been anybody. But, for some reason, they picked me."

The female officer came to the cell and said, "Time is running out." I raised five fingers to her. "Okay," she said.

"Jacob, there's got to be someone, perhaps a neighbor who saw you at home that night. Maybe through the window. Think hard."

"Nobody," he said, shaking his head ruefully. "That's what is so unfair about this. What responsible family man with three kids do you know who has an alibi at midnight? I was home with my kids and wife like I'm supposed to be."

The officer appeared again. "I'm afraid we'll have to be leaving," Luther Z. Jackson said, standing.

"Yes," I said. "There's nothing else you can

tell me?" I asked Jacob, who remained seated, his chin resting on crossed arms.

A grunt was his answer.

"By the way, how is your daughter doing now?" I asked. "Have you been able to speak with your wife?"

"Mr. Jackson arranged for me to make a phone call. My daughter's doing better. We called the doctor that night, and he told us to give her a bath with cool water. I did, and the fever came way down. We all finally got some sleep. My wife brought her to the doctor the next morning, and he put her on an antibiotic." He'd come alive as he spoke of his children. I'd remember that the next time we met as a good way to get him to open up.

The guard unlocked the door, and Jackson and I stepped into the hallway. "I'll be back, Jacob," I said over my shoulder as we proceeded in the direction of the reception area. We'd almost reached it when I stopped, asked permission to say one final thing to him, and without waiting for an answer, quickly retraced my steps, past the prisoner who repeated his sexual slurs to me and to Jacob's cell. "Jacob, listen to me," I said slowly and deliberately through the bars. "You said you spoke to the doctor and he told you to give your daughter a cool bath to bring the fever down. *When* did you speak to the doctor?"

"Late that night. About midnight. I woke him up, but he was nice about it. He said—"

"About midnight," I repeated.

"Yeah. About midnight."

It was his first smile since we'd arrived, and it said many things, all of them positive.

Chapter 14

Attorney Luther Z. Jackson and I lingered outside the jail after leaving his client. "I feel sorry for him," I said.

"You believe him then."

"Yes. Don't you?"

"I want to. I *have* to if I'm to defend him. But I've seen seemingly nice, believable people do not very nice, unbelievable things to others. I'm heartened at his having spoken with Doc Silber that night at the time the murder took place."

"He's a pediatrician?" I said.

Jackson laughed. "Hardly. Silber's an old-timer, a family-type doctor. I haven't seen him in a long time. The only time I do run into him is when I have a case that involves him."

"A case? Malpractice cases?"

"No. Murder, mostly. He's the island's medical examiner. Actually, it's more an honorary position. There's not much murder on St. Thomas, so Doc doesn't have much to do. He's a character actually."

"I just hope he keeps a telephone log, or records his calls," I said. "I'm disturbed at what Jacob said about Walter Marschalk. Walter and I were good friends when he lived in Cabot Cove. That's in Maine. Walter and his wife, Laurie, were neighbors. We spent a lot of time together. I never realized Walter was disliked by so many people."

"Based upon what Jacob said?"

"No. That was just a confirmation of what I've been hearing from many other people. Did you have any dealings with Walter Marschalk?"

"No, although I've heard talk about him. A few local merchants have complained that he doesn't pay his bills promptly. Sometimes not at all."

I sighed. "Well, Mr. Jackson, thank you for allowing me to see Jacob this morning."

"Happy to oblige. And if you come up with any useful thoughts that might help in his defense, please call. You obviously have a head for crime." I wasn't sure I should take his remark as a compliment, but thanked him anyway. He handed me his card on which he'd added his home telephone number, looked up at the sky, and said, "I'd say we're in for rain today."

"Spoken as a lawyer or a weatherman?"

He laughed. "Spoken as a man with an arthritic knee, Mrs. Fletcher. Stay in touch."

I hailed a taxi parked just up the street from the jail and asked to be taken to Lover's Lagoon Inn. The driver's expression was off-putting. "Is there a problem?" I asked.

"I would say so," he said, starting the engine. "The inn is closed."

"I don't think so," I said. "I'm a guest and still there."

"I brought a couple from Lover's Lagoon to the airport this morning," he said. "They told me it was closed. That was why they were leaving. Very angry people."

"The Simses."

"That was their name. Not happy staying in a place all alone and with a bloodstained beach outside their window." He slipped the Toyota van into gear and eased into the flow of traffic.

Although I was silent during the trip back, my mind was hardly idle. If the Simses had left, that meant I was the only remaining guest. Surely, Laurie would close the inn and ask me to leave. I would expect no less.

But the truth was I didn't want to leave. I'd become consumed with the players and events surrounding Walter's murder, and wanted to be there to witness firsthand the denouement. Have a hand in it if possible. There was a limit, of course, as to how long I could stay. I'd arrived on Sunday, and here it was Wednesday morning. I'd planned to stay two weeks, which left me another ten days. Whether the murder would be resolved in that time was conjecture. I knew one thing. I would do everything I could to hasten the process.

Jackson had been right. The rain started as we came over the last mountain, a gentle shower at first, a deluge by the time we pulled up in front of Lover's Lagoon Inn's main entrance. I paid and thanked him for a pleasant ride.

"You might consider staying at another place," the driver suggested. "My cousin owns a very respectable boardinghouse in Christiansted, on St. Croix. Very pretty view of the harbor." Before I could say that I intended to remain a guest at Lover's Lagoon Inn, he handed me a card with a small color photo of his cousin's guest house, and pertinent information. He wrote his name on it. "You go there, you tell her I sent you. Make you a good deal."

"Thank you," I said.

The lobby was deserted, as I expected it to be, with the exception of Maria, the young woman who manned the desk during the day. She was reading a book when I entered, quickly stood, and came to me. "Mrs. Fletcher. Mrs. Marschalk was worried about you."

"I'm perfectly fine," I said. "Where is Mrs. Marschalk?"

"In the kitchen preparing lunch."

"For whom?" I didn't mean it to sound as sarcastic as it came out.

"Staff—what's left of it—and you, of course."

"I understand the Simses have left."

"Yes, and in quite a huff. They demanded their money back. We'll be sending it to them."

"How unfortunate. Well, excuse me. I want to see Mrs. Marschalk."

Laurie was busy stirring something in a bowl in the large, state-of-the-art kitchen when I pushed through the swinging doors. She glanced up, smiled, continued her chore as she asked, "Where have you been?"

"In jail."

She abruptly stopped her mixing, wiped her forehead with the back of her hand, and exhaled. "In jail? Whatever for?"

"I went to visit Jacob Austin."

"Visit? Jacob? Jess, are you all right?"

"I'm fine."

"But why?"

"Curiosity, that's all. Detective Calid called me with the news of the arrest, and I couldn't resist. It's in these genes, I guess."

My reply had been lighthearted, but her face was serious. No. Stern and disapproving was a better description.

"I suppose I should have told you I was going, but I left early to meet Jacob's attorney, a public defender named Jackson."

Laurie sat on a tall metal stool. She seemed unable to formulate her next words. Finally, she said in slow, measured tones, "Jess, that young man murdered my husband. Slit his throat."

"I don't think he did, Laurie."

"You—don't—think—he—did!"

"No. His child was sick that night and—"

"I know full well, Jess, that you write wonderful murder mysteries. But I didn't know you were a trained police investigator. Detective Calid is." I tried to respond but she continued. "He's studied all over the world: Paris, London, the Soviet Union, or whatever it's called these days. Jacob Austin is a ruthless killer. I don't care about his sick child. I don't care about anything except that he be brought to justice." Another attempt by me to speak was summarily dismissed. "Did you know that Jacob made sexual advances to me?"

"No."

"Well, he did. Walter was furious. Add that to the fact that he was lazy, surly to guests, and hated Walter, even threatened him, and you have your murderer."

I knew it was futile to attempt to refute what Laurie had said. And so I didn't. Instead, I said, "I'm sorry if I've upset you. It was silly of me to visit the jail."

"And I'm sorry, too, Jess, for blowing off. I suppose I'm feeling more pressure than I'm willing to admit." She hopped off the stool and picked up the bowl in which she'd been mixing ingredients. "Taste?" she asked, extending the bowl to me.

"What is it?"

"Crab cakes. For lunch. You'll join us, I assume."

"Yes, thank you." I tried a spoon of the delicately seasoned crab and bread crumbs. "Delicious," I announced.

"And lobster for dinner," Laurie said. "Spinach salad with mandarin oranges and a special dressing, watermelon sorbet for dessert."

"An ambitious menu for so few people," I said.

"So few—? Oh, I forgot. I'm hosting a small dinner party this evening. Right here. The inn may be short of guests, but it is my home after all. Please join us."

"I'd be delighted. Who's coming?"

"Some friends. Chris Webb. Senator Jensen. *Former* Senator Jensen. He resigned, you know."

"Yes, I heard. I thought he'd left the island."

"He's back to tie up his legal and financial affairs. There'll be a couple of travel writers, too, who knew Walter. They happen to be next door at Diamond Reef for a conference. They might dredge up tearful memories, but I can handle it."

"Who are they?"

"Travel writers."

"I mean, their names. I met a few of them."

"You did? Oh. Well, there's a woman named Jennifer Fletcher—" She laughed. "Funny, I never thought about you and her having the same last name."

"That is a coincidence."

"And a few others I'm sure you don't know. Cocktails at seven on the patio. We'll have the dining room to ourselves."

"I'll be on time."

"The Simses left this morning. Did you meet them?"

"No, just saw them."

"Unpleasant couple. Almost came to blows with Maria at the desk."

"I'm sorry."

"I'm not. Glad they're gone. Well, back to work, Jess. See you in the dining room in an hour?"

"Yes."

"And Jess, the offer still holds for you to move into the main house. Frankly, having you all alone at the far end of the villas makes me a little nervous."

I smiled. "I haven't felt nervous—yet. But if I do, I'll be here in a flash, my bags packed."

"Good. If you decide to do that, just call for Thomas."

I'd no sooner settled into Villa Number Ten, when Thomas arrived carrying a small telephone answering machine.

"What's this?" I asked.

"Mrs. Marschalk wanted you to have it, Mrs. Fletcher. There's no one at the switchboard now that all the guests—the *other* guests—have gone. I'll hook it up to your phone so you won't miss any messages."

"That's very thoughtful, Thomas. Thank you."

It took him only a minute to make the connections. As he was leaving, he asked, "A drink?"

"A little too early for me, but thank you. I'll wait for lunch."

I opened the top of the answering machine and read the abbreviated instructions on how to record an outgoing message. Confident I understood, I held down a button labeled "ANNC.," and after a tone sounded, said in as formal a voice

158

as I could muster: *"This is J. B. Fletcher. I'm unable to take your call right now, but please leave a message following the tone and I'll get back to you."* I released the button and heard a faint beep. I tapped the "ANNC." button as instructed and heard my voice played back. Not destined to win me an announcer's job but good enough.

I closed the machine's top and took a shower. The phone rang while I was in the bathroom, but there wasn't any need for me to pick up on the bathroom extension. If I'd programmed the answering machine properly, the message would be waiting when I got out.

Sure enough, the message light was flashing when I came to the living room. I pressed "PLAY" and listened: *"This is Maria at the desk, Mrs. Fletcher. I didn't know you'd brought an answering machine with you."* She giggled. *"It startled me. Anyway, I forgot to give you a message before. It's from a Dr. Seth Hazlitt. Please call him."* The number she gave was not Seth's home or office in Cabot Cove. There was no area code. It sounded familiar for some reason. Then I realized it was the main number at Diamond Reef.

Seth at Diamond Reef?

Impossible.

I called and asked the operator if a Dr. Hazlitt was registered as a guest. Her answer was to put me through to his room. "Dr. Hazlitt here," he said.

"Seth? It's Jessica."

"Hello."

"What are you doing in St. Thomas?"

"Escapin' some bad weather back home," he said. "Been cold as a dog, and the wind northeast ever since you left."

159

I smiled. It was good to hear someone talking "Yankee" again. I also had my doubts about his stated reason for having come to the Caribbean.

"So, Jessica," he said, "I thought a few days in the sun would warm these bones."

"Uh-huh."

"Considered stayin' with the Marschalks, but 'cause 'a the trouble there I thought it might be best to stay out of Laurie's hair. Spoke with Jilly, and she recommended this place." Jilly was Cabot Cove's best travel agent.

Somehow, I couldn't picture my slightly corpulent friend fitting in next door with its heavy concentration of tall, tan, young, and lovely singles. Not Seth's style, but he was adaptable to most situations. "Mort with you?" I asked. Usually, when Seth ventured from Cabot Cove, he was accompanied by our sheriff, Morton Metzger. They were best of friends.

"Gorry, no," he said. "Asked him to come along but he couldn't get away. Just me, Jessica."

"Well, this is a surprise, Seth."

"And I promise you I'll stay out 'a your hair, too. What's new with Walter's murder?"

"A few things. I'll fill you in when I see you. *When* will I see you?"

"Whenever you say. I plan to sit about here, get some sun, read the books I brought along with me. You just give a call, and I'll be there."

I considered suggesting he join Laurie and me for lunch, but realized that would be presumptuous. Then I thought of that night's dinner party. I'd tell Laurie that Seth was on the island and see if she wanted to include him in the guest list. "I'm tied up most of the day, Seth. In fact, I have to run out right now but—"

160

"Sounds like you're a mite busy, Jess. Thought you came down here for a vacation."

"And I'm enjoying my vacation. I have some shopping to do. Tell you what. I'll give you a call later this afternoon. Maybe we can catch up for dinner."

"Ayah. I'll be waiting."

I hung up, went to the terrace, and looked down over Lover's Lagoon. A large, flat barge came into view as it rounded a spit of land and chugged slowly into the lagoon itself. I fetched a small pair of binoculars I always carry with me on trips in the event there's time, and opportunity for bird watching, and focused on the barge. A dozen men were onboard, some wearing the uniform of St. Thomas police, others dressed in diving gear. The craft came to a stop and preparations began that soon led to three divers going over the side. I surmised they were in search of the weapon used to kill Walter Marschalk, something I was surprised hadn't happened earlier.

Was it likely that the murderer had tossed the weapon into the clear water of the lagoon? It would have made sense, I suppose, especially if it had been a sudden, impetuous act without premeditation. There are two basic types of murders—those that erupt in a moment of extreme passion, and those planned ahead and carried out with a modicum of precision. If someone had planned to kill Walter, I would have put my money on the weapon being carried away for disposal elsewhere, far from the crime scene.

I watched a few more minutes, then settled in my chair and reviewed my growing list of notes and observations before adding to them.

I'd been remiss in following up on some things.

>> Laurie having filed for divorce.

Having made that notation prompted me to go to the bedroom to retrieve the divorce papers from beneath my clothing in the dresser drawer.

They were gone. Maybe I'd moved them. I searched everywhere, in every drawer. Nothing. Someone had taken them from the villa.

I carefully inspected the room for a sign of someone having rummaged around in search of the papers. Everything seemed in order. Whoever had taken them had been very neat, or knew ahead of time exactly where they were. But who could that be? The chambermaid? She wouldn't have any interest in those papers—unless she'd been instructed by someone to look for them. It was possible that Laurie had eventually learned that I'd accepted the papers from the process server. If so, why not simply confront me? She gave no hint during our brief kitchen meeting that she knew, or was upset. But then again Laurie was proving to be a cool customer in the face of myriad adversity.

>> Find out who took papers from my room.

I jotted down what I remembered of the papers. I hadn't read them thoroughly, had only skimmed them. But I remembered the action for divorce had been filed in Miami, and recalled the attorney' s name—two names actually, a law firm—Karczmit and Bonner. I wasn't certain of the spelling of the first name but it was close enough. An unusual name, I'd thought when first seeing it. And I remembered Bonner because of

162

the double *n*. I notice things like that. Don't ask me why.

I naturally wondered to what extent Walter's extramarital affairs had contributed to Laurie's decision to divorce him. And, of course, there was the question of whether Laurie had become involved with someone else. If so, had that precipitated her decision to end the marriage—and who was it? Chris Webb? Wouldn't be the first time the wife of one partner had ended up with the other. Chris Webb came to mind only because of his involvement with the Marschalks, and because I'd met him.

But if there had been another man in Laurie's life, it could have been anyone. Unlikely I'd ever find out, but I'd keep my eyes and ears open.

>> The doctor Jacob Austin had called the night of the murder regarding his sick child.

His name was Silber. Dr. Silber. Luther Z. Jackson said he would contact him to confirm this potentially lifesaving alibi for Jacob.

>> Check on whether he did. If not, call Silber myself.

>> Accusation by Bobby Jensen that pol spearheading investigation in the Senate on Diamond Reef's payroll. Follow up discreetly at dinner tonight.

One of my previous notes had to do with the murder of a man named Caleb Mesreau, who, according to the newspaper, had refused to sell his tiny tract of land that took in a portion of

Lover's Lagoon. I wrote: *Check newspaper's "morgue" for background on Mesreau murder.*

I recalled Walter's comment that first night at dinner that one of the guests in the dining room was, in reality, a "spy" for Diamond Reef Resort. That was the last I'd seen of him, nor had he been mentioned again. If he was, in fact, a spy for the competition, he should have been considered a suspect. Did the police even know about him? Probably not.

>> Ask Laurie at lunch about the spy.

There were so many things I wanted to ask Laurie. About the divorce papers. About Walter not having accompanied her to Miami as had been originally planned. She'd said something about his not feeling well, and canceling at the last minute. Probably nothing more to it than that. As it turned out, his "illness" proved fatal.

Laurie Marschalk was an enigma to me. Her get-on-with-business-as-usual reaction to her husband's grisly murder was, on the one hand, admirable. At the same time, there was something unnerving about it. She was *too* capable of handling it.

Of course, that represented a judgment on my part, something I had neither the right nor privilege of indulging in. Each of us handles adversity in our own unique way. I remember vividly the days following my husband's death. Assuming that I needed company to fill the lonely days and nights, friends and family insisted upon "taking turns" staying with me. I wanted nothing more than to be alone, but I never expressed it to them. Instead, I dutifully played hostess while tending

164

to the unpleasant chores of making funeral arrangements, and initiating the frustrating, time-consuming business of settling his estate. Did my friends raise an occasional eyebrow at how well I'd "handled it?" Some, perhaps. No matter. I did what I felt I must, and no one else in this world would do it quite the same.

Still, a vision of Laurie preparing gourmet meals for lunch and dinner, and planning a dinner party caused me a pinch of uneasiness. I'd have to get over it.

Chapter 15

My assumption as I headed for the main house was that I would be joining Laurie and remnants of Lover's Lagoon Inn's staff for lunch. But the moment I stepped into the dining room, Laurie came to my side, took my elbow, and led me from the room. "I thought you and I would have lunch alone in the office," she said. "There are a few things I'd like to discuss with you in private."

Thomas was in the process of setting up a rolling table for us—heavy white, starched table-cloth, exquisite silver, cut-glass water tumblers, and, of course, the ubiquitous vase holding an artfully arranged grouping of flaming red Chinese hibiscus. The muted, soothing sounds of Vivaldi came from speakers built into the room's corners.

Thomas had placed two leafy green salads on the table. A bottle of California *Fume Blanc* chilled in a bucket on a stand. The crab cakes, I assumed, were being kept warm beneath a domed silver service cart large enough to contain a small body.

It was picture-perfect for lunch. But there was something else on the table that clashed with the genteel beauty of the setting. The divorce papers!

"Where did you get that?" Laurie asked after closing the door and indicating I was to sit in a chair, in front of which the divorce papers were placed. She was referring to the Lover's Lagoon gold pendant I'd purchased in Charlotte Amalie my first full day on St. Thomas.

I pulled the pendant away from my blouse and held it up for closer inspection. While her eyes focused upon it, mine were fixed upon the legal papers at my place setting. "I bought it in town," I said.

"It's lovely. I haven't seen it before. It's in the shape of the lagoon, isn't it?"

"Yes." It was the first time I'd worn it. Until this moment, I'd wondered whether wearing a gold display of the location of Walter's murder would be in good taste. But I decided before leaving my villa that there was nothing distasteful about it.

"Where did you get it?" she asked.

"A shop in Charlotte Amalie. Peter, the driver you gave me, is related to the owner. Lover's Lagoon Jewelry, I think it was called."

"A cousin."

"Yes."

"He calls everyone on the island his cousin."

"He seemed to have a lot of them."

"If things hadn't gone the way they have, Jess, I'd order a bunch of those pendants for marketing the inn. Not much left to market, though, is there? Hungry?"

"Not especially," I said. "Laurie, I think we should talk about those papers on the table."

She looked down at them, then at me. She smiled. "Oh, those? You've already read them."

"As a matter of fact, I didn't read them. I know I shouldn't have accepted them from the process server, but frankly, I was trying to spare you yet another complication."

"That was sweet of you, Jess."

"No, it wasn't, and I don't think you really consider it an act of sweetness. The fact is I took the papers, read the front page, and put them in a dresser drawer under some clothing. How did you know they were there?"

Her laugh was nervous, and hardly genuine. "I didn't *know* they were there," she said. "Thomas was in your villa making a minor repair, saw them, and thought I would want to have them."

"He was repairing something in my dresser?"

"I don't think you're in a position to question anyone's actions, Jess. After all, you took legal papers that didn't belong to you."

"You're absolutely right, Laurie. But now that this has come into the open, would you like to talk about it?"

"About divorcing Walter? Sure."

We sat and started on our salads. As my friend of long-standing began to talk, it was as though no one else was in the room, the perfect setting for a psychotherapeutic session in which the patient free-associates on a couch while the psychiatrist sits out of sight and offers an occasional grunt.

". . . And so I'd reached a point where I could no longer tolerate Walter's philandering," she said. "I know it isn't good form to speak poorly of the dead, especially when it's your husband, but you might as well know the truth. Walter had an insatiable sexual appetite everywhere but in our own bed. It had been going on for years. At first, I was hurt and felt betrayed, but then I learned to accept it, at least to the extent that it didn't dominate my life." She'd been looking down at her salad as she spoke. She raised her eyebrows as though asking for understanding. I said nothing in the best Freudian tradition. She didn't need any prompting from me.

". . . Which was why we managed to keep the marriage together as long as we did. I focused on those things that were important to me—my cooking and cookbooks, the garden, a few intellectual pursuits that filled the time when Walter was away. He had the perfect job to indulge his *agacerie*. World-famous travel writer trotting around the globe in search of exotic getaways. Always young and attractive female travel writers on the same trips." She snickered. "I even reached a point, Jess, where I not only accepted the situation, I actually began to rationalize his behavior. If I were in the same situation, maybe I would have taken on a lover or two."

I still said nothing.

"Are you wondering whether I did? Take on a lover or two?" she asked.

"No. At least not at the moment, although I did wonder once I saw the divorce papers whether there had been someone else in your life. Frankly, considering the extent of Walter's adultery, I wouldn't be surprised if you had."

"Not this lady, Jess. There was always too much to do to even consider it. With Walter traveling all the time, everything having to do with our life, especially purchasing, designing, and overseeing the building of this inn, fell to me. Sometimes I didn't have time to take a breath, let alone strike up a relationship with another man."

"I can imagine," I said, finishing my last leaf of spinach. "I suppose the irony hasn't been lost on you any more than it has been on me," I said.

"Irony?"

"Yes. Instituting divorce proceedings at a time that coincided with his murder."

Laurie nodded, got up, swung open the dome of the serving cart, and placed a plate in front of each of us. The crab cakes looked and smelled divine. They were accompanied by hash browned potatoes cooked to perfection, and crisp green string beans adorned with walnuts and mushrooms.

We said nothing as we started to eat. I broke the silence by asking, "Is anyone aware besides me that you'd taken action to divorce Walter?"

Her expression said that she thought it was a silly question. "Of course. My attorney, for one."

"Yes, I forgot about him. Anyone besides your attorney?"

"No, and I prefer to keep it that way."

"I can understand that," I said. "Did Walter know you were taking the action?"

"You ask a lot of questions, Jess."

I laughed. "I always have. You know that from being my friend for so many years in Cabot Cove."

"To answer your question, yes, he did. And he wasn't very happy about it. In fact, he told me he would fight me every inch of the way."

I was surprised to hear that. It seemed to me that a man hell-bent on bedding as many women as possible during his lifetime would not be especially upset when his wife of long-standing decided to end the marriage. Then again, I reasoned, Laurie was vitally important to the life Walter had chosen to live, especially once his dream of owning an inn on Lover's Lagoon had become reality. I didn't doubt for a moment that it had been Laurie who'd done all the hard work, and that Lover's Lagoon Inn might never have been possible without her. I suppose my expression mirrored what I was thinking because she said, "You're obviously surprised that Walter was committed to fighting the divorce. Don't be. He knew a good thing when he saw it, the best of both worlds, the dutiful wife holding down the fort and making things happen at home, leaving him free to indulge himself."

I took a few forkfuls of the crab cakes—they were sumptuous, no surprise—before saying, "Are the police aware—?"

Her interruption was sharp. "Did the police know I was going to divorce Walter, and that he intended to fight it? That gives me a motive for having him killed, doesn't it?"

"I wasn't thinking anything like that, Laurie," I said, a lie, perhaps, but necessary at that moment.

"But you'd be right to think it," she said. "If you hadn't accepted the papers from that process server, none of this would be necessary. But since you have, let me be direct. I do not want anyone to know that I had begun divorce proceedings against Walter, or that he was committed to fighting it. Especially the police. I don't need the complication of being viewed as an angry wife with a motive to kill."

I thought a moment before saying, "They won't hear it from me. I assure you of that, Laurie."

"Good. By the way, I tried to call Vaughan Buckley this morning. He's out of town, due back this afternoon."

"Is Buckley House publishing one of your cookbooks?" I asked. Buckley House, a prestigious New York publisher, had been my publisher for years, and its founder, Vaughan Buckley, and his wife, Olga, had become good friends. I wasn't aware that Vaughan had published any of Laurie's culinary efforts, although I did know that Walter Marschalk's last two travel books carried the Buckley House imprint on their spine.

"No. I wanted to get an update on royalties that might be due from Walter's books. I'm looking everywhere these days for funds."

"Yes, I imagine. If you talk to Vaughan, please give him my best. Actually, I'm due to call him to see what he thinks of the manuscript I turned in just before leaving Cabot Cove."

"I certainly will." She glanced at the clock. "Enough of this talk. Finish your lunch. I have a million things to tend to before the party tonight. I'm so glad you can come."

"Speaking of that, I forgot to mention that Seth Hazlitt from Cabot Cove is on St. Thomas. He's staying at Diamond Reef."

Laurie's eyes widened, and she sat back in her chair. "Seth here? How wonderful. Why didn't you invite him for lunch?"

"I didn't think it was my business to," I replied. "But would it be all right if he came to the dinner party tonight?"

"Would it be all right? I'd be angry if he wasn't here. You'll tell him the arrangements?"

"Yes."

"Why is he staying at Diamond Reef?"

"Didn't want to intrude upon you."

"Tell him to check out and get over here. On the house."

"I'll tell him. Laurie, I know you have to run, and lunch was wonderful. But I've been meaning to ask you about the gentleman who had dinner alone in the dining room the first night I was here. Walter was antagonistic toward him. In fact, he told me he wasn't a legitimate guest, but was spying for Diamond Reef."

"Oh, God," Laurie said. "Another thing you didn't know about Walter, Jess, is that as he grew older he developed a terminal case of paranoia. I know the man you're speaking of, a widower who came here for a few days to get over having just buried his wife. Spy?" She guffawed. "Poor Walter. He saw spies behind every tree."

"But you obviously have been engaged in a running battle with Diamond Reef," I said.

"Yes. But that was primarily Walter's doing. The people who own Diamond Reef might not be the most sterling of characters, but they do listen to reason—when reason is presented to them. I've developed a decent relationship with their general manager, Mark Dobson."

"Yes, I've met him," I said, not wishing to elaborate on how much time I'd actually spent next door.

"But Walter would never listen to reason," said Laurie. "As far as he was concerned, this was World War Three. At any rate, forget about spies, Jess. The Cold War is over, both between the United States and the Soviet Union, and between Diamond Reef and Lover's Lagoon Inn."

"I'm relieved to hear it," I said, dabbing at my mouth with my heavy napkin and standing. "Did you see the police this morning diving into the lagoon? I assume they're looking for the weapon."

"I knew they were coming. They had the courtesy to call ahead of time."

"Did they find anything?" I asked.

173

"If they have, they haven't told me. Time to run, Jess." She kissed me on the cheek. "Thanks for understanding about the divorce papers. It will stay between us. Right?"

"Yes."

She used the phone on her desk to fetch Thomas to remove the remains of lunch, and disappeared out the door.

I looked at an ornate clock above her desk. It was almost two o'clock. I'd call Seth and tell him of the plans for dinner, and then head for Charlotte Amalie where I hoped the local newspaper's morgue would shed some light on the three-year-old murder of Caleb Mesreau.

The divorce papers had stayed in the middle of the table throughout lunch, but Laurie had taken them with her. Just as well. Frankly, I wished I'd never seen them, had had the good sense to walk away from the process server.

But wishful thinking, as comforting as it can sometimes be, seldom accomplishes anything. I reached Seth at Diamond Reef and told him to meet me at my villa at six-thirty, had Maria at the front desk call me a cab, and prepared for yet another trip to the busy port city of Charlotte Amalie in search of answers to questions I hadn't even formulated.

Chapter 16

The heavy rain of late morning had been replaced by brilliant sunshine—as well as oppressive heat and humidity. My taxi had air-conditioning, but my driver chose not to use it. I sat in the backseat wiping perspiration from my face and leaning in the direction of the open window to catch any hint of a breeze.

Shoulder-to-shoulder tourists had turned Charlotte Amalie into a sweaty human ant colony and it was slow-going through the clotted downtown area. The driver followed Veteran's Drive, which ran along the waterfront and became Frenchman's Bay Road until the name changed again to Bovoni Road. "What's that body of water?" I asked.

"Bolongo Bay," my driver said. "Caribbean Bay beyond. See over there? St. Croix."

"Yes, I see it."

"Here we are."

He pulled up in front of St. Thomas's local newspaper, which was housed in a one-story white building. As I stood on the sidewalk fishing for money in my purse, I felt as though I was about to melt into the cobblestone. I'd never been so hot in my life. "Don't you ever use your air conditioner?" I asked.

"Oh, yes, ma'am. Whenever it gets hot."

"Whenever it gets—hot. Thank you for a pleasant ride."

"Have a nice day, ma'am."

I pushed through swinging slatted doors and was immediately confronted by a young woman who came around the desk, grasped one of my hands in both of hers, and said, "Mrs. Fletcher. I can't believe how quickly you got here."

"Pardon?"

"You must have had one of our taxi drivers who aspire to drive race cars."

"You know who I am?"

She laughed, as though I'd told a joke.

"Why were you expecting me?" I asked.

More laughter. "For the interview," she said.

"What interview?"

Before I had a chance to say anything else she led me by the hand past the reception desk, through another door, and into a small newsroom in which three people sat in front of computers.

"There must be a mistake," I said, continuing to be propelled to the rear of the newsroom and through an open door to an office where a bear of a man sat behind a desk. He was bald, and wore a white shirt and tie with the collar open and the tie pulled down. His features were heavy and coarse; his nose might have been rearranged from too many stiff left jabs in the ring.

"Adrian," the young woman said, "meet Jessica Fletcher."

He pulled himself to his feet and extended his hand across the desk.

"Mr. Woodhouse is the editor of the paper," she said. "And he owns it."

"Adrian Woodhouse here," he said in a grumbly voice that matched his physique. "What did you do, fly here from Lover's Lagoon?"

I let out a stream of air to lower my frustration level before saying, "Yes, I am Jessica Fletcher, but you shouldn't know I'm here. I mean, shouldn't know that I was coming here. You see, I only came to the newspaper because—"

"Doesn't matter. Delighted to meet you. What say we get on with it?"

"On with what?"

"The interview."

"What interview?"

He looked at me as though I were a dunce. "That's why you're here, isn't it? You got my message?"

"What message?"

"I called to arrange an interview with you for the paper. Famous mystery writer visits island and discovers the body of a *real* murder victim at Lover's Lagoon. Frankly, I didn't know whether you would want to talk about it, but I guess you do."

Had I been a small child, I would have stomped my foot on the floor. "I did not come here to be interviewed about murders or anything else," I said. "I would like to look up something in your morgue."

Woodhouse and the young woman looked at each other with bemused, distinctly confused expressions. "Morgue?" they said in unison.

"Yes, your morgue. By the way, who took a message for me?"

"Your answering machine."

"Oh. Well, I wasn't there to get the message, but I am here to see what you have on a murder that occurred three years ago. A gentleman named Caleb Mesreau."

Woodhouse frowned. "The Mesreau murder?"

"Yes." It suddenly dawned on me that Adrian

177

Woodhouse was the writer who'd done the recent article about the investigation into the Marschalks' purchase of the Lover's Lagoon property. "You wrote the article about Lover's Lagoon Inn," I said.

"That's right. Why do you want to go back into the Mesreau murder?"

"Because your article seemed to hint that there might be a connection between his murder, and the purchase by my friends, the Marschalks, of the property on which they built their inn. Is there a connection?"

"Depends," Woodhouse said.

"Depends upon what?" I asked.

"Depends upon whether you'll let us do an interview with you. You let me interview you, and I'll let you interview me about the Mesreau murder."

"That sounds fair," I said.

"Good." He fell heavily back into his chair. "Me first," he said, dismissing the young woman with a wave of his hand. I took a chair across the desk from him.

He started by asking me questions about my work habits, my approach to plotting murder mysteries—whether I started at the end and worked backward—and whether I considered my novels to be plot or character driven. I'm used to answering these kinds of questions. Lord knows I've been asked them enough times over the course of my writing career. Standard fare for interviewers.

But then he asked about my having discovered Walter Marschalk's body at the beach at Lover's Lagoon. My discomfort level rose with each question asked.

"What did he look like?" this big, gruff island journalist asked.

"Walter? The deceased? Grotesque. Horrible."

"What was your reaction?"

Why do journalists always ask for your reaction to a tragedy? What was I supposed to say, that I broke out a picnic basket and celebrated having found a dear, old friend with his throat slashed?

Woodhouse sensed my annoyance and shifted gears. "I understand you had a conversation with our former senator, Bobby Jensen, and that you visited the accused, Jacob Austin, in jail."

"Yes, I did visit Jacob. A conversation with Senator Jensen? I don't think so."

"From what I hear, you stopped him in the government building and had a long chat with him."

I laughed. "Oh, that. Hardly much of a conversation. He was running to catch a plane, and his staff was anxious that he get moving. I simply introduced myself as a friend of the Marschalks, talked about a few things we had in common, and said good-bye."

The scowl on Woodhouse's face said he didn't believe me, but he didn't press. Instead, he asked, "You're known as a woman who's managed to unravel murders not only in your books, but in real life. What's your read on this one?"

I shrugged. "I don't have a 'read' on this. I wish I did. I know one thing. I don't believe Jacob Austin murdered Walter Marschalk."

"That so? Based upon what?"

"Based upon—my intuition. I understand I'm entitled to intuition by virtue of my sex."

It was his first laugh of the day, a low rumble

that sounded like approaching thunder. He paused as he searched for the next question to ask, which gave me a chance to say, "My turn now?"

"Almost. How were things going between Mr. and Mrs. Marschalk?"

"You mean their relationship?" He nodded. "I'd say it was—fine. Normal."

"What was their 'normal' relationship? Loving? Caring?"

"Yes." Should I mention that Laurie had filed for divorce from Walter, and that I now knew he'd been cheating on her on a regular basis? No, was my answer. To the police perhaps if questioned about it. But not to a journalist. For some reason, journalists believe that, by virtue of their profession, everyone has a duty to be honest with them. I don't share that view. Certainly not where personal lives are involved.

"I hear they were having trouble in their marriage," Woodhouse said.

I shrugged.

"I hear Mrs. Marschalk has been having a fling with someone other than her husband."

"That's news to me," I said. "Who is she rumored to have been seeing?"

He ignored my question and asked, "What do you know about their financial condition?"

"Absolutely nothing," I said.

"My sources tell me they owe a lot of money to bad people."

"Bad people?"

"Organized crime. The Mafia. Loan sharks in Miami."

"Mr. Woodhouse, you seem to have a wealth of information about my friends that I don't have.

180

I really would prefer that you stick to questions about things I know. Like how to write a murder mystery."

"Okay." After a few more such questions concerning my writing career and habits, he took a break to fetch a long black cigar from a desk drawer. He held it up over the desk. "Mind if I smoke?"

"Not at all."

"Most people do mind. At least women. Especially cigars."

"It's your office. I might feel different if we were in my living room."

He lighted the cigar with care and precision, careful not to allow the flame from a gold lighter to actually touch the cigar's tip. After a few enthusiastic and satisfying puffs, he plopped large, bulky shoes on the edge of the desk, pointed at me with the cigar, and said, "Go ahead, Mrs. Fletcher. Your turn. But I reserve the right to ask a few more questions."

"All right," I said, glad the odorous blue smoke was drifting in the direction of a window behind his head. "You wrote the article that appeared earlier this week about the scandal surrounding Lover's Lagoon Inn."

"That's right."

"I found some of your inferences to be without substantiation."

"Such as?"

"For one, the murder three years ago of Caleb Mesreau. Reading the article would lead one to believe that you suspect Senator Jensen and Walter Marschalk of having had something to do with that murder."

He said nothing, simply lowered his chin to his

chest and looked at me through heavy, bushy eyebrows.

"I agree that the fact that Mesreau owned a tiny piece of land that was crucial to the Marschalks going through with their purchase of Lover's Lagoon is gist for speculation. But only that. Speculation. Frankly, when I read the article, I attributed what I considered a lack of solid journalism to a young, inexperienced reporter trying to come up with a sensational story. But now that I've met you, I realize my supposition was incorrect."

"Are you calling me old, Mrs. Fletcher?"

I chuckled. "You certainly aren't a fledgling cub reporter. I assume that you have more in your files than you revealed in the article."

"Maybe I do. Maybe I'm saving it for another day."

"Which, of course, is your prerogative. I would like to see your file on the Mesreau murder. I imagine you covered it extensively, which means your morgue would have it pulled together, presumably under *M*."

"*M* for murder?" he asked.

"*M* for Mesreau. Could I see that file?"

"I don't see why not."

I stood.

"Right now?" he said. "I have more questions for you. Remember our deal?"

"How could I forget it? Let me see the file, and then we'll ask each other some more questions."

He led me to a room in a corner of the building that was piled floor-to-ceiling with files. I'd made extensive use of newspaper morgues before, always with the help of a librarian in charge of the material. But this small newspaper obviously could not afford the luxury of such a person. Woodhouse, who wore many hats, also functioned as keeper of the morgue.

It took him a few minutes to find the file. When he had, he led me back to his office where we took our respective chairs again. I opened the file folder on my lap. After flipping through a few pages, I asked, "May I take this with me overnight?"

"No."

"Then you won't mind if I sit here and go through it? You don't have to stay with me. I promise I won't steal any of the papers."

"If I thought you were capable of that, Mrs. Fletcher, you wouldn't be sitting here in the first place. By the way, someone's throat was slit in your last novel."

I looked up at him. "You read it?"

"Yes. Damn good, up to your usual level of performance. What has Detective Calid told you about the Marschalk murder?"

"Very little, except that he is convinced Jacob Austin is the murderer, and that he expects a confession soon. I doubt if he'll get it. Jacob has an alibi that—" I was instantly sorry I'd begun to mention it. Woodhouse immediately jumped on it.

"What's his alibi?" he asked.

"I think I've spoken out of turn," I said, making a show of going back to reading the papers on my lap.

"But you want *me* to speak out of turn, don't you? What's his alibi?"

"He was in touch with a doctor the night Walter was murdered. He had a sick child, and placed a call to the doctor from his home at approximately the time the murder took place."

"Who's the doctor?"

I couldn't back out now, so I gave him the name of Dr. Silber, which Woodhouse dutifully noted on a yellow pad. "I know Doc Silber," he said. "Has the alibi been checked out by Calid?"

"Probably not. But I think Jacob's public defender, Luther Jackson, was going to follow it up. Do you know him?"

"Jackson? Sure I know him. Good attorney, too good for the public defender's office."

"You look somewhat alike," I said.

"Jackson and me? Why, because we're both too damn fat?"

"Because—oh, just because you do. Sure I can't take this file with me? I promise to guard it with my life, and have it back to you first thing in the morning."

"Sorry, Mrs. Fletcher. It doesn't leave this office."

I quietly resumed my reading. Woodhouse took a few phone calls as I did, and turned to a story he was writing on the computer next to his desk.

I found nothing as I went through the file that had significance regarding Walter's murder.

Until I came across a copy of a letter that had been written to Caleb Mesreau from a law firm in Miami—the law firm of Karczmit and Bonner. The date on the letter was less than a week before Mesreau had been found floating in the bay, his throat slashed, his body tied to an empty oil drum.

In the letter, the attorneys suggested that a fair and equitable price could be arrived at for the purchase of Mesreau's plot of land. They went on to say that the client they represented, who wished to purchase the land, would remain nameless until a deal had been finalized.

Karczmit and Bonner. The law firm representing Laurie Marschalk in her divorce action against Walter.

Woodhouse must have sensed I'd come across something of interest because he asked.

I turned to the next page and shook my head. "No, nothing interesting."

I stayed in Adrian Woodhouse's office for almost another hour. I didn't care whether he was annoyed at my presence or not, although he didn't indicate that he was. He went about his work, leaving the office on occasion, which, I must admit, tempted me to stick in my purse the letter from the Miami law firm. But I didn't succumb. Finally, when I'd gone through every page in the file and had made notes on a small pad, I handed the file back, thanked him, and said I had to be going.

"But I didn't finish my interview with you, Mrs. Fletcher."

"Another time? I'll make myself available," I said.

"How long will you be staying on St. Thomas?" he asked as he walked me to the front door.

"Another week."

"By the way, I need a photo of you. For the story."

"I don't travel with photos of myself," I said pleasantly. "After all, I came to St. Thomas strictly for a vacation."

"And found yourself knee-deep in murder. I understand that isn't unusual for you."

"You're absolutely right, Mr. Woodhouse. It happens with far too frequent regularity. I'll look forward to reading what you write about me. Again, thank you for your courtesy."

I felt him watching me as I went down the stairs and out to the street where I hailed a cab that had just dropped off another passenger. As we drove away, I looked back at the newspaper building and saw Woodhouse still standing in the doorway, filling the door frame actually, hands on hips, his face set in a bulldog expression that would have done J. Edgar Hoover proud.

Somehow, I knew I hadn't seen the last of Mr. Adrian Woodhouse.

Chapter 17

By the time I arrived back at the inn, a powerful wave of fatigue had swept over me, and I planned a fast nap before Seth's six-thirty arrival.

But a flashing light on my answering machine indicated I had two messages. One would be Adrian Woodhouse requesting an interview. I pressed "PLAY," heard Woodhouse's voice asking for the interview, and then the voice of Cabot Cove's sheriff, Morton Metzger, came from the tiny speaker: "Hello, Jessica. Mort Metzger here. Been trying to reach Seth at that resort, Diamond Reef, all day, but they keep tellin' me he's not there. 'Preciate a call when you get a moment."

I returned the call immediately. After initial greetings, I suggested that Seth had probably been out all day sightseeing. "How are you?" I asked.

"Been better, Jess. Joe, my deputy, smashed up the patrol car he was drivin'. Hit a patch of ice, tore through a fence, damn near ran over Billy Cotton's favorite horse, and came to a stop against a big boulder."

"I'm sorry to hear that, Mort. Was Joe hurt?"

"Nah. But you should see that car. Going to take a heap of explaining down at the Town Council. Sure you don't know where Seth is?"

"Yes, I'm sure. But I know where he'll be at six-thirty."

"Where?"

187

"Right here with me. We're going to a dinner party hosted by Laurie Marschalk."

"A dinner party? Hasn't been but a few days since Walter got himself killed."

"Yes, I know," I said, "but don't judge her harshly. She's juggling a dozen problems at once, and is handling them quite well. Want me to give Seth a message?"

"Ayah. Tell him Mrs. Markey had the baby at the hospital. I drove her there myself. Husband's out 'a town on business. Mother and son doin' fine."

"Seth will be delighted to hear that," I said. I knew that Elaine Markey had been going through a difficult pregnancy, which added to my surprise that Seth had chosen to take a vacation. In all the years I've known him, he's seldom left Cabot Cove when a patient was in need. Evidently, he felt Elaine was in good enough hands with a new obstetrician who'd moved to town a year ago, his faith justified by Mort's news.

After Mort and I finished our conversation, I slipped into the Indonesian batik wrap that came with the room, poured myself a glass of pineapple juice from an icy pitcher placed in the room during my absence, and went to my favorite resting spot, the terrace. I stood at the edge and looked out at Lover's Lagoon, expecting to see the police barge still there. It was gone. Had they found the weapon used to kill Walter? I hoped so, and made a mental note to call Detective Calid first thing in the morning to find out.

It was still brutally hot, and the sun was beating down on the terrace. I returned to the room and, for the first time, closed windows and doors and flipped on the air-conditioning. More comfortable now, I sat in a chair and attempted to get back into the book I'd started a half dozen times since arriving on the island. But my mind wandered again; I couldn't focus on the words.

It was five o'clock. I sat at the desk, used my international calling card, and after some static and a delay, reached Buckley House, my publisher in New York. "Vaughan Buckley, please," I said.

Vaughan's secretary of many years, Rhea, a woman I'd grown to like very much, greeted me, asked how my vacation was going, and put me through to her boss.

"Jessica," Vaughan said in his customary ebullient manner. "What are you doing calling your publisher? You're on vacation."

"Yes, I know, but I couldn't help wondering what reactions have been to the manuscript I delivered before taking off for St. Thomas."

"We've only had it for about a week," he said.

"I know, and I suppose I'm growing impatient in my old age but—"

"But—I read the entire manuscript the night I got it. It's wonderful. First-rate. Another winner from Jessica Fletcher."

I sighed. No matter how many books I'd written, and no matter how successful they'd been, I'm always nervous about how people will respond to my latest effort. I suppose all writers feel that way. You pour your heart and soul into a manuscript, and you do it assuming you haven't lost your touch. But you never rest easy until there is confirmation from those you trust, in this case a wonderful publisher, and an astute editorial staff that is always quick to respond, and honest in its responses.

"Enjoying St. Thomas?" Buckley asked.

"I think so, although I've been busier than I would have liked."

"Nothing new there. I was thinking about you when I got the news about Walter Marschalk's murder. I've been on the road at sales conferences since the middle of last week and only caught snippets of news about it."

"I'm staying at their inn," I said. "I was the one who discovered his body."

"You *what*? Discovered his body?"

"Yes."

"And you're staying at Walter's inn? What's it called?"

"Lover's Lagoon Inn."

"Right. How are things there? How are *you*?"

"I'm fine. Things are chaotic, as to be expected. I had lunch with Laurie Marschalk today. She mentioned she'd tried to call you concerning royalties that might be due on Walter's books." There was silence.

"Vaughan?"

"Yes. Sorry. Mentioning Laurie Marschalk and her husband's books brought back some unpleasant, diverting memories."

It was my turn to be silent. As far as I was aware, each of Walter's travel books had sold smashingly well for Buckley House. Unpleasant memories? I asked what he meant.

"Oh, I don't know, Jess. Walter was an incredibly difficult human being. I know I shouldn't be speaking this way about a dead author, but—"

I thought back to when Laurie had made a similar comment about not bad-mouthing the dead. I asked, "Was he *that* difficult?"

Vaughan chuckled. "In all my years publishing

190

books, I've dealt with some of the most frustrating, self-centered, demanding, infuriating authors around. May I just say that Walter Marschalk tops the list."

Another condemnation of my Cabot Cove friend, whom I'd always assumed was a pretty nice guy. The axiom that you can't tell a book by its cover came to mind, appropriate to the moment but too much the pun to be said. "I thought his books were best-sellers," I said.

"They were. They are. Walter had a way of describing a place like nobody else in the business. He could write about a monastery in Tibet, a saloon in Budapest, a Japanese geisha house, or a diner in Des Moines and, by God, you were there. His descriptive powers were without peer."

"So? What difficulties did you have with him? Money? Royalties?"

"All the above, and more. I used to cringe when he called, or stopped by the office. It was as though Buckley House was in business just to serve him. That was the aura he gave off." A soft laugh announced he'd decided to soften his condemnation of Walter Marschalk. "I suppose I'm being unduly harsh," he said. "I had a couple of lunches with Walter that were relatively pleasant. I suppose my view is jaded by that scene I went through six months ago concerning his books."

"Scene? With Walter?"

"As a matter of fact, no. It was with a young writer. You know something, Jess, it just occurred to me that she had your name. Fletcher. Let's see. Her first name even began with J."

"Jennifer Fletcher."

"Good guess."

"No guess involved. I've met Jennifer Fletcher. In fact, she's staying next door to Walter and Laurie Marschalk's inn. It's a resort called Diamond Reef. She's a travel writer attending a conference there."

"Small world. Has she made the claim to you that she wrote Walter Marschalk's last two books?"

"No. Wrote Walter's books? Why would he need someone to ghost his books? You said he was a wonderful writer."

"Let me put it a different way, Jess. Walter's travel books were superb, and I *assume* the words in them came from him—his thoughts, his style, his mind. But according to this young woman— and by the way, Jess, she created quite a scene in my office, threatened to sue, demanded money, was going to the press, a nasty confrontation. At any rate, she claimed she had written Walter's books, every word of them, using material he provided."

"Do you think—?"

"Let me correct that," he said. "She said she and another writer had ghosted his books."

It just came out of my mouth. "Fred Capehart," I said.

"I don't believe this. What have you become, some sort of mystic?"

"Hardly. But Mr. Capehart is attending the conference, too. Evidently there's a relationship between them. What was the thrust of Jennifer's upset, Vaughan? That she and Capehart had written Walter's books but were never paid?"

"Exactly. She claims they had a verbal financial arrangement with him, but that he reneged."

"If that was true, it could make someone pretty mad. Wouldn't you say?"

"Sure."

"Mad enough to kill? Was she that angry?"

I could picture Vaughan sitting back in his chair and holding up his hands. "Nobody should be mad enough to kill anybody" was what he said. "Are you suggesting that this attractive and talented young woman, and her boyfriend, murdered Walter Marschalk to get even for having been stiffed?"

"Nothing of the sort. I'm simply free-associating."

"And your free-associating is pretty damned provocative. What's new with the murder? I assume you're keeping tabs on things in your inimitable fashion."

"Worse than that, Vaughan. I'm determined to get to the bottom of it before I leave this island."

His tone turned markedly more somber. "Mind some advice from an old friend?" he asked.

"When have I ever turned down advice from the erudite and occasionally brilliant Vaughan Buckley?"

He laughed modestly. "Stay out of it, Jess. Move to another hotel on the island, get a little sun—not too much to mar that beautiful fair complexion of yours—and let others solve Walter Marschalk's murder."

"Advice received and under serious consideration," I said, sounding like an airline pilot making an official PA announcement.

"Good," Buckley said. "The next time you see Laurie Marschalk, tell her I'll get a breakdown from the accounting department on royalties that might be coming due on Walter's books. They aren't scheduled to be paid out until spring, as you well know, but if Laurie is in serious financial trouble, maybe I can speed up the process."

"I'm sure she'll appreciate that, Vaughan. Call you when I'm back in Cabot Cove."

I sat on the terrace and chewed on what Vaughan had told me about Jennifer Fletcher and Fred Capehart claiming to have written Walter Marschalk's books. If they had—and if Walter had failed to compensate them as had been agreed—it cast a different light on them regarding his murder.

Was Laurie aware of these claims of authorship?

Did she know Walter had had an affair with Jennifer?

If so, it promised to be a very interesting dinner party.

Seth Hazlitt was characteristically on time. After a friendly hug and kiss on the cheek, we went to my terrace where I'd put out a chilled bottle of white wine and some snacks from the mini-bar.

"You look splendid," I said. "But a little formal for the Caribbean?" He wore a dark blue vested suit, white shirt, muted red paisley tie, and black wingtip shoes.

"It might be a dinner party, Jess," he replied, "but considering that Walter's been dead only a few days, I thought something a little more conservative might be in order. This is a mourning period, isn't it?"

I looked down at my outfit for the evening— a festive, floral cotton skirt and crinkly orange blouse. "Frankly," I said, "you wouldn't know anyone was in mourning. I suppose they do things different here on St. Thomas."

"Good taste doesn't know geographic boundaries," he said sternly, pouring us each a glass of wine and holding his up in a toast. "Here's to seeing you again."

I laughed. "I've only been away a few days."

"Ayah, but when you sit back home hearing and reading about you bein' involved in a murder, it makes it seem a mite longer. Anything new on findin' Walter's murderer?"

"Sit down, Seth. I'll bring you up-to-date."

Which I did, using notes to jog my memory, including a few I'd made immediately following my conversation with Vaughan Buckley.

Seth said nothing as I recounted what had occurred since my arrival on the island the previous Sunday. When I was finished, he rubbed his chin and said, "Sounds to me like it could have been any one of a number of folks who did Walter in."

His conclusion was hardly revelatory. I'd already reached that conclusion myself. "What keeps gnawing at me, Seth, is how many people disliked Walter. He seems to have alienated virtually everyone with whom he came into contact."

"Hardly the Walter Marschalk I remember from Cabot Cove."

"I've been thinking the same thing," I said. "But then again, Walter wasn't there very much. He was always away on a trip. The only time we got together was when he'd come home to do his laundry and pack to leave again. Hard to get to know someone under those circumstances. Wouldn't you agree?"

"Yes, I would agree with that. You say Laurie was about to divorce him, and that he threatened to fight her. Maybe we didn't know Laurie that well, either."

"I keep dismissing that thought, Seth. There may have been tension between them, but Laurie Marschalk is no murderer."

"But what if there was someone else who'd be affected by Walter's refusal to grant her the divorce?"

"Another man in her life?"

"Ayah."

"She denies being involved with anyone."

"Except you say there's this partner, Webb, and these attorneys up in Miami who tried to buy the property from that fella they found dead three years ago."

"The same attorneys that were handling her divorce."

"Seems possible to me that this fella, Webb, might have had something to lose if Walter didn't agree to the divorce."

"Such as?" I asked.

He shrugged. "Just thinking out loud." He checked his watch; it was a few minutes before seven. "Time for us to get movin'?" he said.

"Give me a minute to freshen up." I checked my makeup in the bathroom mirror, then pulled my blue blazer from the closet but realized I hadn't bothered to sew the missing button back on. I tossed a white scarf around my neck, received a nod of approval from my Cabot Cove friend, and we headed off.

I was certain Seth would be out of place in his dark suit. But it turned out that I was the one inappropriately dressed. Everyone was in black or navy. Laurie wore a floor-length black silk dress that clung to her every curve. Pamela Jensen, Senator Bobby Jensen's wife, a pretty woman tottering on the verge of overweight, wore a black suit, frilly white blouse, and abundant jewelry. Even Jennifer Fletcher, whom I assumed traveled light with clothes appropriate only to the destination, was in slacks and a cotton sweater of a somber gray color.

The men were in suits—gray or blue. Only Chris Webb tipped his hat to the island culture by wearing white shoes, and a wide, vividly colored tie on which flamingos of varying hues played on his chest.

When Laurie greeted Seth and I at the door to the dining room, I noticed Fred Capehart huddled in a corner with Jennifer Fletcher. The minute he saw me, he quickly left her side and disappeared through doors leading to the kitchen.

"What a sight for sore eyes," Laurie said, taking in Seth from head to toe, then hugging him.

"Bet you didn't expect to see me here," he said.

"No, I certainly did not. When Jess told me you'd arrived on St. Thomas, I was thrilled. Now we can have a proper party, just like back home in Cabot Cove."

Laurie had transformed the dining room into an elegant setting. Individual tables had been placed together in the center of the room to form one long one at which a dozen places had been set. Thomas, wearing a white shirt, starched white jacket, and black bow tie, manned a small bar in one corner. A young man sat on a stool in another corner cradling an acoustic guitar as though it were a living thing, and played familiar classical melodies.

The ambiance was as refined and pleasant as one might expect when attending an intimate state dinner party at the White House, or Buckingham Palace.

Laurie surveyed the room, said, "Let me see. I know you have met some of these people, Jess, but they're all strangers to you, Seth. Come. Let me introduce you."

And so we made the rounds. I'd met everyone, including a couple of guests whose presence was a surprise, to put it mildly—Mark Dobson, Diamond Reef's general manager, who no longer wore a cast on his leg, and who greeted me like a long-lost family member; and the hulking, imposing owner of the St. Thomas newspaper, Adrian Woodhouse. I'd had the feeling I'd see him again, but never dreamed it would be this soon, or in this circumstance.

The only person in the room I'd not met was a tall, strikingly attractive woman who Laurie introduced as Nadine Kodner. "My mentor," she said. Nadine had shoulder-length gray hair, and I judged her to be about forty-five. She and Laurie might have been sisters. "Nadine has written several cookbooks," Laurie said. "Not only is she a wonderful writer, she can cook rings around me."

Nadine shook off the compliment. "Don't you believe it," she said. "Nobody can hold a spatula to Laurie Marschalk."

Introductions completed, Seth settled into a conversation with Bobby Jensen and his wife, and I accompanied Laurie to the bar. "I didn't know you were that friendly with Mr. Woodhouse, the newspaper owner."

"Adrian? A marvelous man." I suppose my face reflected my puzzlement over her view of Woodhouse. After all, he'd written a scathing article that all but accused Walter Marschalk and Senator Bobby Jensen of having illegally conspired to buy the Lover's Lagoon land, and perhaps to have even arranged the murder of an old man in order to bring that about.

"You're thinking about the article he wrote," Laurie said, reading me perfectly. "He's already apologized for it, and is planning to do another piece exonerating us of any collusion or conspiracy."

I looked over her shoulder and saw Woodhouse and Jensen sharing a hearty laugh. Incestuous little group, I thought as I carried my drink to where Seth had stationed himself near the guitarist. A waiter passed carrying hors d'oeuvres, and Seth had stacked a half dozen of them on a small plate.

"Enjoying yourself?" I asked.

"As well as can be expected," he replied. "Fill me in on these people. Some of the names I recognize from what you told me back at your room."

I quickly outlined relationships, and mentioned that Adrian Woodhouse was the one who had written the damning article about the Marschalks and the inn.

"Laurie's pretty friendly with a fella who wrote bad things about her."

"So is former Senator Jensen," I said.

I was about to approach Woodhouse when Laurie announced, "I think it's time we sat down.

Otherwise, we'll all be too drunk to enjoy dinner."

Name cards were at each place setting. I was to sit between Jennifer Fletcher and former Senator Bobby Jensen. Jensen's wife, Pamela, was to his right; Fred Capehart was to Jennifer's left. Laurie took her place at the head of the table, with Seth on her right hand, Chris Webb on her left.

I wasn't keeping count, but it seemed a great deal of liquor had been consumed during the cocktail hour. Thomas had been perpetually busy concocting a variety of island drinks, although I noted that Chris Webb, Adrian Woodhouse, and Bobby Jensen eschewed such fancy creations for glasses of amber or white liquor on the rocks.

No matter what the form of alcohol, tongues had been noticeably loosened, with the exception of Jennifer Fletcher and Fred Capehart, who said little. I attempted to initiate conversation with her but she responded only with one word answers, and ignored me for the entire dinner. There was a festive air in the room, and much laughter. When had Walter died? Monday night at about midnight. It had been less than forty-eight hours since his death. His cold body still sat in a police morgue pending the investigation of his murder. Yet, a lighthearted, spirited *party* was in full swing, hosted by his widow. I glanced over at Seth and gathered he was thinking the same thing.

When Mort Metzger had questioned a dinner party so soon after Walter's demise, I'd defended Laurie. But now, as I sat at the elaborately set table and heard the tinkle of ice cubes in drinks and hearty laughter, the soft strum of the guitar and the buzz of happy conversation, I knew I'd have difficulty mounting such a defense again.

As though Laurie sensed what both Seth and I were thinking, she tapped her water glass with a fork, stood, wineglass in hand, and asked for our attention. It took a few moments for conversation to die down. Once it had, she held up the glass and said, "Lest anyone wonder at my having this party so soon after Walter's death, let me say that I've always been someone who believes in celebrating life, not death. In fact, Walter and I had an agreement. A party such as this, with dear friends, would be held as soon as possible after the death of either of us. Somehow, I know he's listening in on us—and approving." She turned to where Thomas stood erect behind the small bar. "Please," she said.

He came to Laurie's side carrying a glass of liquid. Laurie took it from him, held it up to the light, smiled, and said, "I can almost see Walter's smiling face in it. This was his favorite drink, the Lover's Lagoon cocktail. Each of you has one. Please join me in a toast to a remarkable man, world traveler, best-selling author, devoted husband, and innkeeper without peer."

"Here, here," Chris Webb said, slurring the words.

We all lifted our glasses. I, of course, knew that Walter was hardly a "devoted husband," and that the only reason he hadn't been served with divorce papers was because he'd died. I suppose I should have admired Laurie for putting on such a facade for her guests. In fact, I did feel a certain admiration. But she'd laid it on a little thick for my taste.

Seth, who also knew the real situation between

the Marschalks because I'd told him, looked as though he'd bitten on a sour candy. I'd checked Jennifer and Fred Capehart's reaction when Laurie mentioned Walter's status as a best-selling author. Their expressions were blank, noncommittal.

Laurie had remained standing, thrusting her Lover's Lagoon drink at each person who offered his or her own response to the toast. She tapped her glass again and waited until she had everyone's attention. "Now," she said, "I have an important announcement to make." She looked at Mark Dobson, whose satisfied smile indicated he already knew what she was about to say. "Mark, would you help me make the announcement?"

He joined her at the head of the table. "In fact," Laurie said, "maybe it's more appropriate for Mark to be the one to tell you this wonderful piece of news."

He looked at each of us before saying, "I suppose we can consider this a wedding announcement. At least an engagement notice."

There were puzzled looks and a few gasps, me included. Wedding announcement? An engagement? Mark Dobson and Laurie Marschalk?

"Now that I have your attention," he said, laughing at what he considered his clever opening, "let me explain. Just about all of you here know that over the past three years, Diamond Reef and Lover's Lagoon Inn have not been on what you'd call friendly terms. All-out war more accurately sums it up. But I'm here tonight to announce a truce, a cease-fire. Hostilities have been concluded."

I must admit that a wave of satisfaction, even

happiness swept over me. Some people applauded. Chris Webb, who by now was overtly drunk, knocked over his wineglass as he extended his hands to clap. Newspaperman Adrian Woodhouse nodded in obvious satisfaction at what he'd just heard.

The only two people at the table who did not openly display pleasure at the announcement were Jennifer Fletcher and Fred Capehart.

It was Laurie's turn. "Diamond Reef and Lover's Lagoon Inn will soon be one," she said. "It will take a while"—she laughed—"for the lawyers to sort things out. But when all is said and done, and the tees have been crossed, and the eyes dotted, the lagoon, which Walter always said was the most beautiful small body of water in the world, will be available to all who stay at Diamond Reef and its exclusive private resort, Lover's Lagoon Inn."

There were more toasts and congratulations. Laurie's final comment was directed at Adrian Woodhouse: "I told you it would be worth your while to come here this evening, Adrian. You have a scoop. Dinner is served."

It certainly was. The lobster was baked and stuffed with a "five-spice stuffing" that perfectly complemented the rich, succulent lobster meat. The salad was almost too pretty to disturb by eating it. Sourdough bread was served with red pepper jelly that I thought I wouldn't like, but did—to the tune of two slices. And the watermelon sorbet was augmented by what Laurie announced was "Magen's Bay mocha mousse pie" that defined decadence. All in all, a Lucullan feast from the hands of a highly skilled chef, Laurie Marschalk, aided no doubt by her

203

"mentor," Nadine Kodner, who I learned during dinner lived in New York, had a house on St. Thomas where she spent her winters, and taught cooking classes in Switzerland, France, and Spain.

After dinner was cleared, Thomas served a variety of brandies from a small serving cart. I'd decided to make a point of speaking with Jennifer Fletcher and Fred Capehart before the evening was out. They'd been obvious in their desire to avoid conversation with me, but I was not about to be put off, not after the conversation I'd had with Vaughan Buckley.

But that plan was thwarted because the minute they got up from the table, they announced to Laurie that they had to leave. I observed the three of them as they chatted near the door. If Laurie was aware that Jennifer had been one of the other women in Walter's life—or knew she and Capehart had ghostwritten his books and hadn't been paid for their efforts—she displayed nothing to indicate it. They talked and laughed freely, good old friends ending a pleasant evening.

I looked for Seth. He'd left the room, probably in search of the rest rooms. Jennifer and Fred kissed Laurie on the cheek, and they, too, were gone. A minute later, Seth returned through the same door through which Jennifer and Fred had exited.

"Did you see where the young couple went?" I asked.

"The other Fletcher lady and her boyfriend? Ayah."

"Where? I mean, did they get into a car out front?"

"She did, but not until they had some harsh words for each other."

"They argued? What did they say?"

"Couldn't quite hear everything they said, Jess. I didn't want them to know I was listenin' so I stayed around a corner after coming out 'a the men's room. It had something to do with plans for tomorrow. She didn't seem keen on what he was suggestin'."

"What was he suggesting?"

"I never did catch that. All I know is that he's goin' to leave a message for her back at Diamond Reef."

"I see." I looked at the other guests who'd stayed. One other person was missing. Chris Webb, the Marschalks' partner. "Did Jennifer get into a taxi?" I asked Seth.

"Nope. A big black Mercedes driven by that Webb fella."

Another clandestine meeting in Charlotte Amalie? I'd almost forgotten about that. Should I suggest to Seth that we head for town for a little pub crawling? Or to browse a museum that was closed? I almost did, but Adrian Woodhouse came to where we stood and launched into a monologue on the problems of modern medicine. It was for Seth's benefit, I assumed, and I was proud of my friend for not engaging in what could easily have become a quarrel over his profession.

"More brandy, Mrs. Fletcher?" Thomas asked.

"Thank you, no," I said.

"I will," Woodhouse said.

"I believe I will, too," Seth said. His expression told me he felt he needed it to ride out

Woodhouse's increasingly strident condemnation of medicine.

"Excuse me," I said, leaving them alone with the subject. I looked for Laurie but didn't see her. A few minutes ago I'd seen her talking with Nadine Kodner, who was now engaged in a conversation with Mark Dobson and Pamela Jensen. I joined them.

"Quite a surprise you announced," I said to him. "I think it's wonderful."

"About time," he said.

"I agree," said Nadine. "So silly having two such wonderful places at war with each other."

"My sentiments exactly," said Dobson. "Lover's Lagoon is a special place on this earth. Now, more people will be free to enjoy it."

"Where's Laurie?" I asked.

"In the kitchen, I think," answered Nadine.

"Time for us to leave," I said. "I wanted to say good-bye."

"I'll get her," Nadine offered.

"Don't bother. I know my way around the kitchen." I laughed. "At least in a directional sense. Excuse me."

I pushed open the swinging doors and stepped into the kitchen. The staff had cleaned up and was gone. Two small lights cast tentative illumination over the large room. I saw no one and was about to return to the dining room when I heard a noise from a narrow corner created by a wall, and the side of a huge walk-in refrigerator. I took a few steps in that direction. The noise was louder this time. It was a woman's breathy, passionate voice that whispered, "I love you."

Before I could turn and beat a hasty retreat, Laurie Marschalk and Bobby Jensen stepped into the light. He quickly wiped lipstick from his mouth with a towel that was folded on a stainless-steel preparation table. Laurie pulled down her silky black dress that was up to her hips.

And then they saw me.

"Excuse me," I said. "Seth and I are leaving."

I disengaged Seth from Adrian Woodhouse, said good-bye to the others, and we were on our way out the dining room door when Laurie emerged from the kitchen. She glared at me across the room.

"Let's go," I told Seth, fairly pulling him from the room.

"What's the matter?" he asked.

"Tell you later."

As we headed for my villa, Bobby Jensen emerged from a back door to the kitchen and circled around in the direction of the inn's main entrance.

"Somethin' wrong, Jess?" Seth asked. "You look like you've seen a ghost."

"You know I don't believe in ghosts," I said. "But I do believe in justice. Come on. We have some things to do."

"*We?*"

"Absolutely. If I can work on my vacation, I don't see any reason why you shouldn't work, too."

Chapter 18

The answering machine was flashing when Seth and I entered my villa.

"Meant to ask you about that before," he said as I pushed "PLAY." "Unusual for a hotel to provide answering machines to the guests."

"Very unusual," I said. "Listen."

"Good evening, Mrs. Fletcher. Detective Calid here. I would appreciate it if you would call me when you return. No matter the hour." He left his home number.

"Who's he?" Seth asked.

"The detective in charge of Walter's murder investigation," I said. "Sit and relax while I call him."

He answered on the first ring.

"I hope I haven't woken you," I said.

"No chance of that, Mrs. Fletcher. I assume you haven't heard the news about Jacob Austin."

"No, I haven't. I've been out all evening, just returned. I trust it's good news."

"Only that it were, Mrs. Fletcher," he said through a deep, pained sigh.

"I'm listening," I said, tossing a quick glance at Seth, who'd settled his body in a chair, his attention upon me.

"Your friend, Jacob—"

I interrupted. "My friend? What makes you say that? I'd hardly call him my friend."

"I understand you were quite friendly with him during your jailhouse visit."

"Does visiting someone in jail automatically bond them as friends?" I asked, aware that this banter was keeping him from delivering what was obviously more important news.

"Well, Mrs. Fletcher, that you weren't friends might make what I have to say a little easier to accept. Austin committed suicide tonight in his cell. Wrapped a sheet around his neck and hung himself."

"Oh, my God."

"I'm sorry, Mrs. Fletcher."

"But he had an alibi. Did you check with Dr. Silber about the call Jacob made to him the night of the murder?"

"Yes, I did, Mrs. Fletcher. Unfortunately, Dr. Silber had no record of that call."

"No record? A medical doctor has no record of a patient's call?"

"Mrs. Fletcher, I know you're upset, and I apologize for being the bearer of this news. Whether Dr. Silber should have kept a record of the young man's call—and whether that call was actually made—is beyond the scope of this conversation. I am simply extending the courtesy of letting you know."

He was right, of course. He had no obligation to call me with the news. I thanked him, then asked, "Might I come see you in the morning? At your office?"

"Well, I—I have meetings all morning."

"Afternoon? At your convenience."

"Perhaps it would be best to call in the morning. I'm sure time can be arranged."

"Thank you. I will. By the way, Detective Calid, did your divers find what they were looking

209

for today in Lover's Lagoon? The murder weapon?"

"No. Might I be so bold as to suggest something to you, Mrs. Fletcher?"

"I'm always open to suggestions, Detective."

"Try to resist the temptation to become further involved in this murder. Go home. Come back to St. Thomas another time, another year when it will live up to its reputation as a vacation paradise."

I looked to Seth again, who hadn't taken his eyes off me. He'd suggested the same thing. Go home.

"I may do just that," I told Calid.

"Fine. As for me, it's been a trying and tiring day, as you can imagine. Good night, Mrs. Fletcher."

"Good night."

"Bad news, I take it," Seth said when I hung up.

"Shocking is more like it. Jacob Austin, the young man accused of murdering Walter, has hung himself in jail."

"Maybe you were wrong," said Seth. "Maybe he *did* kill Walter."

"I suppose that's always a possibility. But if I were a betting woman, I'd wager he didn't."

I filled him in on Calid's claim that Dr. Silber had not kept any record of a call from Jacob. "Does that sound reasonable to you, Seth. You're a doctor. If a patient called you at midnight concerning a sick child, would you not have kept a record of it?"

"Possible. Sometimes you get so many calls like that you forget to note it in the records. 'Course, I wouldn't *forget* such a call. When did

210

you say it was made? Monday night? That's only two days ago. Unless this Dr. Silber is losin' his memory, he sure would have remembered such a call."

"Of course."

"Did he prescribe anything for the child? Antibiotic? Cough medicine?"

"Let me see. Jacob told me his wife took the child to see Dr. Silber the next morning, and she was put on an antibiotic."

"That's easy enough to check. Why don't you—?"

"I have a better idea. Why don't *you* stop in and see Dr. Silber tomorrow morning? You know, a little doctor-to-doctor talk."

"Ayah. I'll do it. You said you had work to do."

"Tomorrow. Right now I need to sort out my thoughts, get them on paper, and grab some rest. I suggest you do the same."

"I get the distinct feeling I'm being told to leave."

"Nothing of the sort. It's just that I'll be occupied and—and if you hurry, you might not miss the limbo contest at Diamond Reef."

His first expression was that I was being serious. Then he broke into a smile, and I joined in it. "Good night, Seth," I said, kissing him on the cheek. "Let's meet for breakfast in the morning at Diamond Reef."

"Eight?"

"Seven. I have a feeling it will be a long day. An early start will help. See you in the coffee shop."

An hour later I'd added copious notes to my notebook and was ready for bed. But first I called the message desk at Diamond Reef. "This is J. B. Fletcher, Room twelve-oh-two. Any messages for me?"

"No, Ms. Fletcher."

"Thank you."

I climbed into bed wondering whether guilt associated with representing myself as Jennifer Fletcher would get in the way of my falling asleep. It didn't, because I wouldn't let it. After all, my name *is* Fletcher. Content with that rationalization, I said aloud, "Sleep!"

And I did.

Chapter 19

Seth and I arrived at Diamond Reef's coffee shop at the same moment, entering through different doors. We were seated at a table for two by a window, and menus were placed in front of us.

"Sleep good?" I asked.

"Ayah. You?"

"Eventually. After my vision of that young man hanging in his cell faded with fatigue. I'm hungry. Didn't think I would be."

"Let's see what they can rustle up to take care 'a that."

I ordered a fruit plate with cheese, croissants, and tea; Seth ordered bacon and eggs. As he sometimes quipped, "They'll be selling cholesterol pills ten years from now. The medical profession doesn't know nearly as much as it pretends to."

"Speaking of the medical profession," I said, "ready to visit Doctor Silber?"

"Yes. I'll call his office the minute we leave here. Still not sure what you want me to find out."

"Just whether he did, or didn't, keep a record of Jacob's call that night. And if he didn't, why can't he at least remember it? I won't rest until I know for certain that Jacob made that call."

"I'll do my best."

"And Silber is, according to Jacob's public defender, St. Thomas's medical examiner. Sort of an honorary title, according to Jackson, but

Silber would be the one to sign Jacob's death certificate. I'd like to learn more about that from him, too."

"All right. What's on your agenda today, Jessica?"

"See Detective Calid to learn more about Jacob Austin's death from his perspective. I also want to visit Jacob's family."

"Why?"

"To offer my sympathy."

"Hardly seems necessary. You don't even know them."

"True. But I did meet him. I reached out to him. I saw him cry, first out of depression, then with joy when he remembered having called the doctor about his child. If nothing else, Seth, I think the family would appreciate a visit from someone who believed in his innocence."

"I suppose you're right. I heard you ask the detective last night whether they'd found the murder weapon. Take it he said they hadn't."

"That's right."

He slid half glasses lower on his nose and fixed me like a professor. "You know, Jessica," he said, "I'm goin' along with you because I happen to be here, and because you're one of my favorite people, to say nothing of my favorite author. But don't consider my willingness to collaborate to mean I agree with what you're doing."

"What in the world am I doing?" I asked, my attempt to sound startled falling flat.

"Tryin' to solve Walter Marschalk's murder. That's police business. None 'a yours."

"And I shall remember that," I said as breakfast was served.

We left the coffee shop and stood in the lobby,

prepared to go our separate ways. "Excuse me," I said. "I have to check for messages."

"Here? At Diamond Reef?"

He followed me to a bank of house phones. "Jessica, why are you using the phone? Just go on over to the desk and—"

I shushed him with a finger to my lips, and he stepped away. The message operator came on the line. "J.B. Fletcher here," I said. "Room twelve-oh-two. Any messages?"

"Yes, Ms. Fletcher. There's one from Mr. Capehart."

"Oh, What is it?"

"He left an envelope for you."

"Oh, my," I said. "I'm at a public phone and won't be back all day. Would you be good enough to open it and read what's in the envelope?"

"Sure."

From my vantage point, I could see her across the lobby as she plucked the envelope from a honeycomb of boxes and tore it open. "Here's what the note says, Ms. Fletcher: *'Jenn—Set for Pettyklip at three; provisions arranged; don't be late; Fred.'*"

"Set for *where* at three?"

"Pettyklip." She spelled it for me. "I assume he means Pettyklip Point. On the east end, near Red Hook. Where the ferries leave for St. John."

"Of course. Would you please leave a message for Mr. Capehart and Ms. Fletcher."

"Mr. Capehart and—Ms. Fletcher?"

"Yes. Fletcher. My niece, J. Fletcher." I laughed. "We're always being confused for each other. Please tell both my niece and Mr. Capehart that the razor used to murder Walter Marschalk,

215

the owner of Lover's Lagoon Inn, has been found by the police."

"It has? Where?"

"I really shouldn't say, but they found it in Lover's Lagoon, just a few feet into the water from where the body was discovered."

"Wow!"

"You will see that they each get that message."

"Of course."

I hung up and faced Seth, who stood a few feet away with arms folded across his chest. "What was that all about?" he asked.

"Nothing. Just something I had to do. Tell you what. Let's meet at my villa at one. You'll have seen Dr. Silber, and I'll have made my rounds. We'll order lunch in."

"All right."

"Oh, one other favor, Seth. Before we meet, would you call the message desk here at Diamond Reef, say you're Fred Capehart, and ask for your messages?"

"I don't believe in that sort 'a thing, Jess."

"Just this once? After all, you're on vacation."

"I'll think about it."

"I can't ask for more than that. See you at one."

I stopped at my villa before heading off for the morning. To my surprise, Laurie was waiting there for me. She'd let herself in and sat in the living room.

"Good morning," I said.

"I'll get right to the point, Jess. I'm a patient person. I accept human foibles, quirks, obsessions. But I've run out of patience with you."

"Why?"

"Your snooping. I resent you peering around corners, asking questions, playing sleuth."

"I'm sorry, Laurie, but that's certainly not what I've been doing. If you're upset about last night, my coming into the kitchen and finding you and—"

"You found nothing, saw nothing."

"Fine. But know that I came into the kitchen simply to say good night. I wasn't snooping."

She raised her hands in a gesture of frustration, then slapped them sharply on the top of her thighs. It sounded like a bullwhip being snapped. "All right. I'm sorry," she said. "But I've been under an immense strain, as you can imagine. This alliance with Diamond Reef is vitally important to me. Bobby—Senator Jensen and I were in the kitchen discussing a very sensitive issue that must be resolved to insure the deal going forward."

"Of course. I understand."

She came to me, smiled, and placed her hands on my arms. "Maybe when all the dust has settled, we can sit down like old times, schmooze, drink coffee, laugh, swap stories."

"I'd enjoy that," I said.

"In fact, Jess, when this is over, I think I'll make a trip to Cabot Cove just to get together with all the old friends. Beginning with you, of course."

"I'd like that. Have you been told that Jacob Austin hung himself last night in his cell?"

"No."

"It's true," I said. "I'm on my way to find out more about it."

"Then he *was* guilty," she said.

"I don't think there's necessarily a cause and effect at play. I still don't think he killed Walter."

"What else can you take from his killing himself? God, Jess, apply a little logic."

Rather than debate it, I asked, "Had you been told anything by Walter, or others, that the young couple at dinner last night—Jennifer Fletcher and Fred Capehart—claim to have ghostwritten Walter's books and weren't paid for their efforts?"

"Wow!" She raised her arms to the heavens and vigorously shook her head. "You are something else, Jessica Fletcher. Any other gossip I should know about?"

"I'm sorry," I said.

"You are not one bit sorry, and you know it. What a preposterous statement to make. Walter's books ghostwritten? My God, he must be turning in his grave—or will once he's in it. Where did you hear such garbage?"

"It doesn't matter."

"Oh, it certainly does, Jess. If someone is slandering Walter and the work he left behind, I want to put a stop to it. Jennifer and Fred, you say? They're making such claims?"

"Yes."

"*They* told you that?"

"Not directly. I spoke with Vaughan Buckley at Buckley House. Jennifer and Fred made that claim to him six months ago."

Her overt, physical display of shock and dismay had vanished. Now, she went to the entrance to the terrace and looked out.

"I know you're upset, Laurie," I said, coming up behind her. "And as hard as it might be for you to believe, I'm not meddling. I didn't call

Vaughan in search of such information. It just came out during our conversation."

"I think Mr. Vaughan Buckley and I had better have a little talk," she said.

"Yes. I think that would be in order."

"Well, I suppose there's nothing more to talk about. Have you thought about going home, Jess?"

"Many times."

"I think you should. I'm closing the inn until all the details are ironed out with Diamond Reef. Sorry your vacation coincided with this mess."

"I am, too," I said. "I'll talk to Seth later today about heading back to Cabot Cove. If he isn't ready, maybe I'll stay the rest of my vacation next door."

"As you wish."

"I would enjoy a final lunch or dinner with you, Laurie. Could we do that? Today? Tomorrow?"

"Today's out of the question. I have some business on St. John. Why don't we save it for when I come to Maine."

"That's a fine idea. I'll let you know what I've decided."

"I have to run. Again, Jess, I'm sorry things turned out this way."

"No apologies necessary. Have a nice trip to St. John."

I was pleasantly surprised when my taxi driver turned out to be Peter, who'd driven me to Charlotte Amalie my first full day on St. Thomas. He was as unfailingly pleasant and courteous as he had been that first day. "Where to today, Mrs. Fletcher?" he asked after I'd gotten into the front passenger seat of his Jeep.

"Charlotte Amalie. Police headquarters."

"You enjoy that sort of thing, don't you?" he said as he pulled away.

"What sort of thing?"

"Government. Last time, it was the Senate building."

"Yes, I suppose I do. Have you heard anything about a young man named Jacob Austin killing himself last night in jail?"

"Oh, yes. On the radio this morning."

"Did you know him?"

"Yes. We went to school together."

"They say he murdered Walter Marschalk."

"I don't think so."

"You don't think he was the killer?"

"No, ma'am, although I don't have any specific reason for saying that. Just that Jacob wouldn't kill somebody. Not in my opinion. He had a temper for certain, and I know he told many people how much he hated Mr. Marschalk. But kill him? I don't think so."

As we passed the house in which Peter had been born, he slowed down and honked the horn, which brought a few people onto the porch to wave.

"My momma's been sick," he said.

"I'm sorry to hear that, Peter. Nothing serious, I hope."

"No. Just a flu."

"Has she seen a doctor?"

"Momma?" He laughed. "Last person she'd go see is a doctor. Like she always says, if you want to stay healthy, stay away from doctors."

I laughed, too. "I suppose that's a good rule to follow—with certain doctors. By the way, do you know a physician on the island named Silber?"

His laugh was more sinister this time. "Ol' Doc Silber? Sure, I know him. Everybody does."

"Is he a doctor your mother would stay away from—in the interest of good health?"

"Yes, ma'am, that he is."

"He doesn't sound like a very good doctor."

"He was once, I hear. 'Til the rum caught up with him."

"He's an alcoholic?"

A knowing laugh came from Peter. "That is what you would call an understatement," he said.

"And he's still allowed to practice medicine?"

"He hasn't killed anyone as far as I know," Peter said, negotiating a sharp turn and barely avoiding a head-on collision with a van. "People still go to him—poor people—'cause they've been going to him for years."

"How old is Dr. Silber?" I asked.

"Oh, must be seventy, I guess."

St. Thomas's medical examiner is a seventy-year-old physician with a drinking problem. Small wonder a midnight telephone call might be forgotten. Seth was in for a challenging morning.

I asked Peter to wait for me as I went into police headquarters in search of Detective Calid.

"He's at the jail," I was told.

Which was our next stop. As I walked through the front door, I spotted Luther Z. Jackson, attorney-at-law, bantering with the pretty young female officer at the desk.

"Excuse me," I said.

"Mrs. Fletcher," Jackson said. "I wasn't expecting you."

"I know. I should have called. Detective Calid called me last night with the news about Jacob."

221

"Dreadful what happened to him. Hard to fathom."

"He must have been extremely despondent," I said. "Which is hard for me to accept. When I left him yesterday, he was upbeat after remembering his call to Dr. Silber."

"Yes," Jackson muttered.

"I assume you called Dr. Silber," I said.

"I—I meant to." He focused on his shoe tops.

Somehow, I knew he hadn't made that call, and there was nothing to be gained by berating him. Chances are he would have met with the same alcoholic memory loss as had Calid.

"Is Detective Calid here?" I asked.

He was happy I changed the subject. "I saw him a few minutes ago," he said. "He's in with the warden."

"Any ideas about this?" I asked.

"Ideas? No. Jacob was obviously distraught and took his own life."

"No qualms, no reservations?" I asked.

"I don't think so." He frowned, touched my elbow and guided me from the desk to a corner where we wouldn't be overheard. "What are you suggesting, Mrs. Fletcher, that there might have been foul play?"

"That hasn't crossed your mind?"

"Why should it? I haven't seen or heard anything to lead me to that conclusion."

"I haven't either," I said. "But it certainly is convenient, isn't it? Jacob dies, and everyone views it as an admission of guilt. That gets whomever did kill Walter Marschalk off the hook. Case closed. Very neat."

Jackson looked over his shoulder, leaned

closer, and asked, "Who are you accusing, Mrs.
"Whoever benefits most from Walter's death."

He shook his head. "That doesn't hold up for
me," he said. "Few people would have had access
to Jacob's cell. Someone off the street, someone
in his family, business associates wouldn't be able
to enter the building, the cell, and physically hang
him up by a bedsheet."

"I agree," I said. "But what if someone had
the clout to *arrange* for this to happen?"

"Arrange for it to happen?"

"Yes. A guard is paid off to slip something into
Jacob's food or drink. While he's unconscious,
he's strangled, then propped up with a sheet
around his neck."

"No offense, Mrs. Fletcher, but are you sure
you aren't plotting your next novel?"

"I hope not," I responded. "By the way, a
friend of mine from back home, Doctor Hazlitt,
is on St. Thomas. He's visiting with Dr. Silber
as we speak."

"A little late, I'm afraid," Jackson said.

"For Jacob? Yes. But I can't help but feel that
Dr. Silber *did* receive that call from Jacob. And
if he did, at least Jacob's name can be cleared
posthumously, for his family's sake."

"All I can say, Mrs. Fletcher, is that I wish you
well. Frankly, your friend will probably come up
empty-handed. Doc Silber is—well, let's just say
his best days are behind him."

I smiled. "Old demon rum will do it every
time."

"You know about Doc's drinking?"

"Yes."

Detective Calid suddenly appeared from the

recesses of the jail. He saw me and quickened his stride in the direction of the front door.

I caught up with him. "Might I have a few minutes with you?" I asked.

"Not now, Mrs. Fletcher. I told you to call the office for an appointment."

"Just one question, Detective. Just one."

"Okay. One question."

I asked, "Who killed Jacob Austin?"

His expression said he hadn't heard me, or hadn't understood the question. But I knew he had—heard me and understood. "Jacob did," he said.

I shook my head.

"As you wish." He started to walk away, stopped, turned, glared at me, and closed the gap between us. "I've been very patient with you, Mrs. Fletcher. I've told you things about this case that you had no business knowing. I called you with the news about the kid's suicide. But I'd be less than honest if I didn't say you have become a stone in my shoe."

"Better than rocks in your bed," I said.

"What?"

"An old song."

"I'm not interested in songs, Mrs. Fletcher. I'm interested in doing my job. I'm leaving. I have other more promising appointments. But I have one question for you."

"Yes?"

"Why are you spreading rumors that we found the murder weapon?"

"I wasn't aware that I had."

"You have. I heard."

"From whom? Who told you that?"

"That's a second question. You promised to ask only one. Good-bye."

"Good-bye, Detective Calid. Thank you for your time."

"And stop spreading rumors, Mrs. Fletcher. I don't need it."

I watched him leave the building, then looked to where Luther Jackson and I had been talking. He, too, was gone.

Peter stood next to his Jeep as I left the jail. He opened the door for me and climbed behind the wheel.

"Have you heard a rumor that the police had found the weapon used to murder Walter Marschalk?" I asked.

"No."

"I'm surprised. It seems to be all over St. Thomas."

"Where to next?"

"Jacob Austin's home. Do you know where his family lives?"

"Yes, I do."

"Then that's where I want to go."

And, I silently mused, I wanted to know who had called Detective Calid with my planted rumor that the weapon had been found. Jennifer Fletcher or Fred Capehart? I wasn't aware they would know whom to call.

If it wasn't either of them, to whom had they passed the rumor?

Laurie Marschalk?

Senator Bobby Jensen?

The Marschalks' partner, Chris Webb?

Newspaper owner Adrian Woodhouse?

Other travel writers staying at Diamond Reef?

Diamond Reef's general manager Mark Dobson?

I wanted to know because, somehow, my instincts told me that Walter's murderer was the same person.

Chapter 20

Jacob Austin's widow and three children lived in a small, neatly kept house on a busy road in a town called Fortuna, on the western side of St. Thomas. The house was, like most houses on the island, made of white stone and had a red tile roof. A jungle gym and slide dominated the tiny front yard.

A number of cars lined the narrow street on both sides. Grieving family members and friends, I assumed. My resolve to visit had weakened. Would the unannounced presence of an unfamiliar tourist be viewed as presumptuous, even rude? I hoped not as I took a deep breath, got out of the Jeep, and approached the front door. The dog lifted its head, gave me a tentative bark, and went back to sleep.

Voices came from inside the house. I knocked; a small child responded. "Hello," I said. "Is your mother home?"

She ran from the door yelling, "Mommy! Mommy!" A moment later her mother faced me. "Yes?" she asked. She was a pretty, slender young woman with brown hair that fell softly to the shoulders of a simple green-and-white cotton dress. "I'm sorry to intrude at a time like this," I said, "but I wanted to express my sorrow at what happened to your husband."

"I don't understand. You knew Jacob?"

I started to explain, but the moment I mentioned my name, she smiled and said, "Yes,

Mrs. Fletcher. Jacob told me about you when he was allowed to call yesterday afternoon. He said—" Her smile broke into a tearful grimace. "He said you were trying to help him."

"I'm afraid I wasn't very successful," I said.

"Please, come in."

The interior of the house was as neat as the outside. The furniture wasn't expensive, but had obviously been chosen with care to fit the small confines of the living and dining rooms. One thing was certain. Jacob Austin's wife was a meticulous housekeeper, and mother. The three children, even the one-year-old, were dressed in pristinely ironed clothes.

A dozen people milled about the living room, where Mrs. Austin—I realized I hadn't learned her first name—had set a table with fruits, cookies, and a large coffeepot. One visitor wore a clergyman's collar, another the white garb of a hospital worker.

"I'm sorry, Mrs. Austin," I said. "I don't know your first name."

"Vera," she said. And then she introduced me to her family and friends: "Mrs. Fletcher is the woman who visited Jacob in jail and tried to help him."

I was warmly welcomed. After a cup of strong, spice-flavored coffee was handed me, the clergyman, Father Wallingford, asked about my visit with Jacob in the jail. "Did he seem especially despondent to you?" he asked.

"No," I answered. "But I saw him in the morning. Perhaps—"

He shook his head. "I visited with Jacob right after dinner," he said. "He seemed in fine spirits, thanks to you pointing out that Doctor Silber might be able to provide him with an alibi."

"But I understand the doctor didn't provide the alibi," I said.

"Exactly right, Mrs. Fletcher. Unfortunately, he was unable to."

Vera Austin joined us. I said to her, "Jacob told me you took the sick child to Doctor Silber the next morning, and that he prescribed an antibiotic."

"I did take Clarise to him, but he didn't prescribe the drug. He gave us some from his own supply. Doctor Silber usually does that to save his patients money. He gets them from the big drug companies, I think."

I sipped my coffee as others joined us. "A friend of mine from home, a doctor, is on St. Thomas," I said. "He's gone to talk with Doctor Silber this morning to find out whether—"

"He won't find the doctor there this morning," a stout woman, who'd been introduced as Vera's aunt, said.

"He won't?"

"No. Doctor Silber is my neighbor. He left bright and early this morning for the States."

My frown reflected my confusion. "Was this a sudden departure?" I asked.

The stout woman laughed. "Oh, yes. A sudden retirement, too."

"Retirement?" I said incredulously.

"Doctor said he's going to live with relatives in the States. Having things packed up and shipped for him. That's what he told me. Gave me his cat, Swizzle Stick, to keep. I have two of my own, but what's one more, I say?"

"Yes, what's one more," I repeated, my voice now heavy with defeat.

I looked at Vera Austin. "Jacob did make that call the night Walter Marschalk was murdered?" I said.

"Of course. I stood next to him when he called the doctor."

"And now the doctor has vanished. Just like that. Sudden. Permanent. I wonder who got to him."

"Pardon?" the stout woman said.

"Just thinking out loud," I said.

"I don't know what we'll do for a doctor now," Vera said. "The children loved him. He made them laugh."

I walked away and looked through a window into the front yard where the two older children now climbed on the jungle gym. Vera came to my side, saw them, and yelled for them to come in and change their clothes if they were going to play outdoors.

"I really must be going," I said. "Again, I am so sorry about Jacob. If it's any solace, at least you and your family know he did not commit any crime."

It was the first time a hint of bitterness crept into her voice. "Yes, Mrs. Fletcher, *we* know he didn't. But everyone else on St. Thomas believes he did, and that his suicide confirms it." She began to cry. "At least he left us insurance. Strange, isn't it, that the man they say he killed, Walter Marschalk, is responsible for us receiving enough money to live on for the rest of our lives."

"I don't follow," I said.

"Jacob's life insurance policy at the inn. Mr. Marschalk paid for the policy."

"But Jacob was fired, I heard Mr. Marschalk fire him."

"I don't know how those things work," Vera said, wiping tears from her cheeks. "I just know that Mrs. Marschalk called and told me about the policy. I never even knew Jacob had it."

"Well, I'm glad there is at least that for you," I said.

"I'd better get the children," Vera said.

I had nothing else to say, no comforting words, no perspicacious thoughts to help ease the pain. I left the house, climbed into Peter's Jeep, wiped away a tear that slowly ran down my cheek, and said, "Let's go back to the inn."

"You okay, Mrs. Fletcher?"

"No, I am not okay, but that isn't your problem. Please. I just want to go home."

Chapter 21

I heard the knocking but couldn't relate to it. It was from a faraway place, someone else's door. I forced my legs over the side of the chaise lounge, rose unsteadily to my feet, crossed the living room to the door, and asked, "Who is it?"

"Seth."

"Seth." I looked at my watch. Three past one. He undoubtedly had arrived at one sharp, and had been knocking for three minutes. I unlocked the door.

"Gorry, Jessica, you look terrible," he said when he was inside.

"Thank you very much. I fell asleep on the terrace and—it doesn't matter. Sorry to keep you waiting."

"I was beginning to worry." He followed me to the terrace.

"Have a seat," I said, changing direction toward the bathroom. "I need to wake up."

When I returned, Seth was looking down over Lover's Lagoon. "A beautiful sight," he said into the air.

"Yes, it is. Get you a drink?"

"Thought we were havin' lunch. I'm a mite hungry."

"That's right. I forgot. I'll try to get something brought up, but I doubt if I can. Laurie told me she's closing the inn until details of the merger are worked out with Diamond Reef. There's probably no one in the kitchen."

"Let's go next door."

"That's one of many things I love about you, Seth. You're a clear and decisive thinker."

We ordered club sandwiches and iced coffees at the same table at which we'd had breakfast. Neither of us was very talkative. Since I knew all about Dr. Silber skipping town—and that's exactly what I considered his abrupt departure to be—there was no need for Seth to explain his lack of success in ferreting out the imbibing physician.

I, of course, espoused my theory on why he'd left St. Thomas, summing it up with, "He was bought off."

"Serious charge" was Seth's reply. "Who?"

"Whoever is comfortable having the world think that Jacob Austin is a killer. Show me that person, and I'll show you the real killer."

"Reasonable to assume, I suppose, that whoever paid the doctor to leave town is the same person who paid to have the young fella murdered in prison. *Providing*, 'a course, that either event happened the way you think it did."

"You're right on both counts," I said.

It dawned on me as we sipped the chilled coffee that I'd never told Seth of the furtive meeting that night in Charlotte Amalie between Chris Webb, Jennifer Fletcher, and Fred Capehart. And so I did.

Seth pointed to a window that looked out over the coffee shop's outdoor dining area. I followed the direction of his finger, adjusted my vision to compensate for glare on the glass, and saw what he was pointing at. Chris Webb, Jennifer Fletcher, Fred Capehart, and Laurie Marschalk sat at a table. Standing over them was Diamond Reef general manager Mark Dobson.

"Looks like they're doin' business in the daylight these days," Seth said.

"Looks like it."

"I knew they'd be havin' lunch together."

"Oh?"

"Ayah. I did what you asked me to do, against my better judgment, I might add."

"What did you do?"

"Called the desk and asked for Fred Capehart's messages."

"And?"

"He had two. One was that the murder weapon was found in Lover's Lagoon. The other was from Laurie. Said she had to talk with him immediately, and set up the lunch they're havin' here today."

"I think we should go out and say hello," I said.

The sun had been shining brightly when we arrived for lunch. Now, as we stepped outside, the sun was obscured by metallic gray clouds that had begun to settle low over the island. A brisk breeze whipped in from the east; umbrellas over the outdoor tables flapped.

Laurie and the others saw us approaching and abruptly ceased their conversation. Mark Dobson, a broad, professional smile on his face, greeted us a few feet from the table. "Hello, Jessica," he said. "Dr. Hazlitt." He extended his hand to Seth.

"We just finished lunch inside," I said, "and thought we'd stop by to say hello."

"Hello, everyone," I said when we reached the table.

My greeting was halfheartedly returned.

"Looks like a live storm brewin' up," said Seth.

"They're forecasting a norte," said Dobson.

"Norte?" I said.

"Norther," he explained. "We get them occasionally in winter. They blow down from North America and can get pretty nasty."

"Like a hurricane?" I asked.

"Different," Dobson said. "But equally destructive at times."

"Good thing they found the murder weapon before the storm hits," I said lightly, looking at Laurie.

Her answer was a smirk, and a barely discernible shake of her head.

"You don't agree?" I asked.

"You've been reading too many of your own murder mysteries, Jess," she said.

"Maybe I have," I said, laughing.

"They didn't find the weapon," Laurie said. "I spoke with Detective Calid."

"We have to go," Jennifer said. She stood and told Capehart with hard eyes that he, too, was expected to leave. He got the message and walked away with her.

"On your way to St. John?" I asked Laurie.

"Yes."

"You look especially lovely today, Mrs. Fletcher," Webb said. "The vacation must be agreeing with you."

"It's beginning to," I said. "Well, we're off for the afternoon."

Webb looked to the sky, which had lowered even more as the wind increased. "Hope your plans aren't for a picnic," he said, smiling.

"No," I said. "Just some sightseeing. A little rain won't bother us."

"Enjoy yourselves," Webb said. He took Laurie's arm and they, too walked away, leaving Seth and me standing alone at the now vacant table. We looked at each other. "Nervous crew," he said.

"You noticed."

"What's this business about the weapon bein' found? The detective told you last night it hadn't been."

"You know how rumors get started."

His grin was all-knowing. "I think I know how this one got started," he said. "Where to next? Are we really going sightseeing?"

"Absolutely. I thought an afternoon on St. John would be a pleasant choice. I've been reading about it in my guidebook. Small—only nine miles long—peaceful, quiet, a nature-lover's paradise. You with me?"

"Not the sort 'a weather for nature walking," he said.

"Nonsense. I predict the sun will be shining by the time we get there. Game?"

He winced against raindrops that fell on his face. "Just hope you're as good a weather forecaster as you are a writer, Jessica."

Chapter 22

The taxi driver who responded to our call from the inn was an older woman with orange hair, and who wore a crimson dress adorned with a dozen strands of pearls. Her name was Olive, she said.

"Pettyklip Point," I said after we'd settled in her yellow Toyota van.

"Thought we were going to St. John," Seth said.

"We are. After we check out something at Pettyklip Point."

"Not much to check out there," Olive said over her shoulder. "If you're going to St. John, the ferry leaves from Red Hook."

"That's close to Pettyklip Point," I said.

"That it is." She boosted her windshield wipers to their fastest speed to keep up with the ever-increasing rain that made visibility difficult.

"Understand there's a norte on the way," Seth said. I smiled. When in Rome—or St. Thomas—speak like the natives.

"That's right," said Olive. "The brunt of it's supposed to be here around six."

"Not a good day to be out on the water," Seth offered.

Olive laughed. "All the shipwrecks around the islands attest to that," she said. I silently wondered how many automobile wrecks on St. Thomas attest to the mistake of *driving* in a "norte."

As we came down the north coast on Route 30, it became increasingly narrow, hilly, and winding. The view to our left, I knew from previous rides, was beautiful—in good weather. This day, all was shrouded in a gray mist, and further obscured by the downpour.

Eventually, Route 30 became Route 32, and after passing such landmarks as Benner Bay, East End Lagoon, and Compass Point, a sign said we were now on Red Hook Road. I breathed a sigh of relief. I'd cracked open the window in search of fresh air. I'd begun to feel nauseous; a few more minutes on the road and I might have been very sick.

We reached Pettyklip Point, and Olive parked in front of a building whose sign announced the rental of water sports equipment. Business was nonexistent. To the right was a dock to which a dozen craft of varying sizes and shapes were secured.

"Looks like you're lucky," said Olive as Seth paid her. "Skies are brightening."

Seth and I looked up. Sure enough, the cloud cover had lifted somewhat, and the rain had diminished to a steady drizzle.

We stepped beneath an overhang on the aquatic rental building. "What are we doin' here?" Seth asked. "The ferry to St. John leaves from Red Hook."

"I just want to stand here a few minutes," I said. I looked at my watch. It was two-forty five. According to Capehart's message to Jennifer, they were to meet at three.

"All right," Seth said, "but there doesn't seem much to linger for. Just some tied-up boats and—"

"Wait," I said, urging him back against the building. He followed my gaze to the black Mercedes that had come around a corner a hundred yards away and that slowly approached the dock.

"That's Mr. Webb's car," Seth said.

"Right," I said. "Let's see who's with him."

Webb came to a stop at the dock, and all four doors opened. Webb got out from behind the wheel. Laurie emerged from the front passenger seat. From the rear stepped former island senator Bobby Jensen, and Diamond Reef general manager Mark Dobson.

The foursome headed toward the end of the dock, which took them out of our sight. I checked my watch again. Five minutes before three. Were Capehart and Jennifer Fletcher already on the dock waiting for Webb and his entourage? "Come on," I said, pulling at Seth's sleeve.

The dock was longer than I'd first thought. Tied up at its far end was a long, boxy cabin cruiser whose polished wood hull testified to a pre-fiberglass heritage. Webb and the others stood next to a gangplank leading from the dock to an opening to the deck. Jensen kept checking his watch; they all appeared to be anxious for something to happen. Where were they headed? I wondered. St. John? Presumably. Laurie had said she was going there this afternoon. But why all of them? A meeting? That would be the rational explanation for it. They seemed to meet a lot—at night in downtown Charlotte Amalie, lunches, dinner parties, and now on a boat.

I was debating whether to approach them when I caught a fleeting glimpse of Jennifer Fletcher, who'd stepped from the boat's cabin to the deck, said something to the group on the dock, then ducked back inside. I couldn't hear what anyone said, but I had the impression that the exchange between Jennifer and Webb's contingent wasn't pleasant.

I decided against making our presence known to them, content to simply watch at this juncture. Maybe one of them would do something, make a move that would turn on the cartoonists' light-bulb over my head. Since leaving Jacob Austin's house and widow, I'd been plagued by a nagging, unstated, infuriatingly elusive thought. What was it? What demon idea was lurking far back in my brain, too far to readily be brought to the front where I could act upon it? "We just going to stand here?" Seth asked.

"Yes."

"Why don't we go up and say hello again, like at lunch?"

"Because I want to—look."

Seth held a flattened hand over his eyes and squinted. "Look at what, Jessica?"

"Did you see the face in the cabin window?"

He leaned forward, as though the additional few inches would enhance his vision. "Nobody in the window."

"Not now," I said. "But there was. A face I won't soon forget. Uh-oh. Here they come."

We retraced our steps to the building that rented snorkeling and scuba diving equipment, and positioned ourselves at its side. I peered around the corner. Webb, Jensen, and Laurie were leaving the dock and walking toward Webb's black Mercedes. Dobson had evidently remained behind, probably had boarded the cabin cruiser.

"Don't let them see us," I said.

We waited until they'd driven off before leaving our vantage point and returning to the dock. A young man tossed mooring lines to the cabin cruiser. Catching them on deck was Fred Capehart.

I looked around. Most vessels tied to the dock were unoccupied. But there were two that appeared to belong to a man who sat in a director's chair. A sign at his feet read: "JERRY'S BOATS FOR RENT."

"How are your sea legs?" I asked Seth.

"My sea legs? What in the devil are you talking about?"

"Let's go to St. John."

"That's where I assumed we were going when we came here."

Capehart had pushed off from the dock, and the cabin cruiser slowly moved away under engine power. I went to the man with the rental boats and said, "Looks like the weather is breaking."

He looked to the northern sky. "Maybe," he said.

"My friend and I would like to rent one of your boats."

"Jessica, I—"

"Don't we, Seth?"

"I don't understand what we're—"

"Can we? Rent one of your boats? Jerry?"

Jerry screwed up his face. "You know how to run a boat?" he asked.

I don't even know how to drive a car, but Seth, who'd spent a good portion of his life on the waters of Cabot Cove, had just sold his own boat the previous summer.

"Of course," I said. "Don't you—doctor?"

"You're a doctor?" Jerry asked.

"Ayah," Seth replied.

"And a good sailor?"

"Well, I—"

"The best," I answered for him. "They're pretty boats," I added, hoping to soften him.

Seth left my side and looked down at the boats. "Nice rigs," he said. "Had a Boston Whaler myself till recently, only it wasn't this big. Twenty-two footer?"

"That's right, mon." Jerry stood. "The weather's not so good," he said. "You can see that for yourselves. What do you want a boat for?"

"Just to take a ride," I said.

Jerry looked at Seth. "Just for a ride," Seth said.

"All right. But just for an hour. Local. Stick close to shore. You got some form of ID?"

"Plenty." I whipped out my credit cards, and Seth extended his driver's license. I handed Jerry a handful of cash. "A deposit," I said. "We'll be back in an hour."

Minutes later, Jerry had pushed us away from the dock and into the shallow, greasy water adjacent to it. Seth handled the craft as though he did it for a living, and we were on our way.

"Stay local," Jerry shouted after us. "Stick close."

I waved and smiled. "Don't worry," I said. "We will."

Once clear of the dock and other boats, Seth idled back and turned to me. "Now that we're out here, Jessica, just what was it you had in mind?"

"Follow that boat," I said.

242

"What?"

"The cabin cruiser that just left. Follow it."

"But the fella said—"

"Please. Just for a few minutes."

"All right." He gunned the large outboard engine from his position at the center console, and we roared off in pursuit of the cabin cruiser, whose running lights were barely visible in the distance.

I stood next to Seth at the center console and held on tight as the Whaler lurched through the choppy water, rising up on the swells, slapping down hard in the troughs. It was exhilarating and frightening at once. Salt spray stung my face as we gained on the cruiser.

"Dumbest damn thing I've ever," Seth shouted. "Look out there." The northern horizon had turned black. We'd enjoyed the proverbial lull before the storm. There it was, the "norte" in all its fury.

"Let's go back," Seth said.

He was right, and I knew it. "Just a few more minutes," I said, my words carried away on the increasing winds. I narrowed my eyes and trained them on the cruiser, whose form came and went in the mist and churning sea.

"Look!" I yelled.

Seth saw it, too. Something had fallen from the cabin cruiser's deck. A large bag? A box? A body?

The cruiser suddenly turned hard right and increased its speed. Seth looked to me for our next move. I pointed to where we'd seen the object go overboard.

It wasn't until we were almost on top of Jacob Austin that his position was known to us. He was flailing in the rising and falling sea, bobbing on top like a cork, then disappearing beneath the surface. Seth chopped back on our power. We both looked for something to throw to the drowning man. "Use that," Seth said, indicating coiled line attached to a circular buoy. Holding on to a low metallic railing, I inched forward to the front of the boat. Jacob had just come up from beneath the water. His desperate eyes locked on mine. I tossed the buoy to him, and he grabbed it, hugging it to his body. I wrapped the line around a cleat on the deck as Seth came forward to help. Together, and despite the boat thrashing about in the tumultuous water, we managed to pull Jacob to the boat and helped him come up over the side.

Seth immediately returned to the console, revved the engine, and regained control of the craft. "Where to?" he shouted.

"Land," I said. "Any place safe and dry."

Chapter 23

Detective Calid, Seth, Jacob, and I sat in the detective's office at police headquarters. We'd gone directly there after arriving safely back at the dock at Pettyklip Point and returning the Boston Whaler to a relieved Jerry.

"All right, Jacob," Calid said. "Let's go over this one more time."

Jacob, wrapped in a heavy blanket provided by Calid and still in a mild case of shock from his ordeal, said, "I already told you what happened."

"Tell me again," Calid said. "Sometimes I'm a slow learner."

"Okay," said Jacob. "It was a plan, a scheme. When you arrested me for killing Marschalk, I knew I wouldn't be convicted because I didn't do it. I never killed nobody."

"I already understand that part," Calid said. "But what happened later? After you were arrested?"

"That's when I got the note from Mr. Dobson."

"Diamond Reef's general manager," I said.

"Yeah. Right. Butch, the guard gave it to me."

"This note." Calid held up a wet piece of paper that Jacob had been carrying in his clothing.

"Yeah," Jacob said. "That note."

Calid had read the note to us: *"I can get you out of jail, and you'll make lots of money."*

"So, what did you do?" Calid asked.

"I talked to Butch and said I'd be interested

in finding out what Mr. Dobson meant. Butch arranged for me to use a telephone to call him."

"Dobson."

"Yeah, Dobson. He told me that if I would go along with having people think I died, I'd be set up in the States with fifty thousand dollars, and my family would be moved there."

"And you decided to go along with it," I said.

"Sure. Once I heard that Doc Silber wasn't going to provide an alibi for me, I figured I probably would be convicted—even though I didn't do it. So I agreed. Dobson sent me another note—I lost that one—and told me I'd be taken from the jail at night, hid someplace, and then taken to the States. Everybody would think I committed suicide."

I reached across the short gap between us, placed my hand on Jacob's shoulder, and said, "And that's where you thought you were going today."

"Yeah. I really trusted them."

I looked at Calid. "You say this guard, Butch, is now in custody?"

Calid nodded. "You were here," he said, "when I called over to the jail. He was on duty, but he's in a cell now. The warden says he's blabbering away about how all he did was deliver a note to Austin, and take him out of the jail that night."

"He's verifying what Jacob has been saying so far?"

"That's right. Go on, Jacob," Calid said. "What happened next?"

The young man shrugged. "They put me in a basement room over at Diamond Reef. Like a storage room. They put a bed in there and brought me food. I was supposed to stay there until today when I was going to the States."

"Did your wife, Vera, know any of this?" I asked.

He shook his head.

"She knew about the fifty thousand dollars," I said.

"She did?"

"I visited Vera at your house this morning. You have a lovely family, Jacob. Vera said Mrs. Marschalk had called her about a life insurance policy Mr. Marschalk had bought for you."

"There was no life insurance," he said angrily.

"I know," I said. "Walter Marschalk had told me the first day I was on St. Thomas that he wasn't about to provide such benefits to his employees. I'd forgotten that when Vera told me about the money. But then I remembered it later this afternoon. I saw your face for a fleeting instant through the window of the boat you were on. That's when I realized there was a grander scheme at foot."

"And good thing you did," Seth chimed in. "If you hadn't, Mr. Austin here would be a very dead young man."

"I know it must be painful to have to tell it again," I said, "but what happened on the boat this afternoon?"

"They threw me overboard."

"They?" Calid asked.

"Mr. Dobson and that Fred guy."

"Fred Capehart?" I said.

"Yeah. Both of them. Capehart was the one who showed me the razor."

We sat up a little straighter. He hadn't mentioned any razor the first time around.

"What razor?" Calid asked.

"Mine. The one I bought as a present for my grandfather."

"Fred Capehart had it?" I said incredulously.

"That's what convinced me to go through with the plan. Once I was in that basement room at Diamond Reef, I decided not to do it. I didn't want people to think I'd killed myself, or that I was a murderer. So I told Dobson I wouldn't. That's when Capehart arrived. He had the razor and said my fingerprints, and Marschalk's blood were on it. If I don't go along, he'd turn it over to the police."

Calid and I looked at each other.

"Looks like you've got your murderer," Seth said to the detective.

I asked Jacob, "Did Fred Capehart indicate he was the one who'd killed Walter Marschalk?"

"He was the one," Jacob said coldly.

"How do you know?" Calid asked.

"I heard him tell that girl, Jennifer. They argued a lot. She was real mad that he killed Marschalk. I thought he was going to kill *her* on the boat today, he was so mad."

"I certainly hope not," I said. "What about the others? Mr. Webb, the Marschalks' partner, Senator Jensen, Mrs. Marschalk?"

Jacob shrugged. "I heard them talking together once about some deal. I didn't understand any of it."

"Did any of them know that Fred Capehart had murdered Walter Marschalk?" I asked.

Another shrug.

Seth asked, "Any idea where they went on that boat after they tossed you over to the sharks?"

"No. Oh, wait a minute. They had a map out in the cabin. Somebody had drawn lines on it."

"Lines to where?" I asked.

"Puerto Rico, I think."

"That's about it," Calid said. "You'll have to give an official statement to a stenographer," he told Jacob.

"Not again," Jacob said. "I'd like to see my wife and kids."

"You'll see them soon enough," Calid said. "Wait here."

The detective walked us to the lobby. "I suppose I owe you an apology," he said.

"An apology for what?" I asked.

"For not listening to you more closely. Because of you and your friend here, we don't have another murder on our hands today."

"But we *do* have a few unanswered questions," I said.

"We'll get Capehart. I'll send an all-points to Puerto Rico and the States as soon as you leave. With this storm, they may not make it anyway."

"At least Jennifer Fletcher might not make it," I said. "Detective, do you have any idea why a group of such distinguished people—a former senator, a businessman like Webb, and my good friend, Laurie Marschalk, would have gone along with this? No, I take that back. They evidently were in on the planning from the beginning. Why?"

"That's a question I intend to ask when I interrogate them, Mrs. Fletcher. In the meantime, I suggest you just forget about the whole affair, relax, read—or write a book—and leave the rest to me."

"An excellent suggestion," said Seth, shaking Calid's hand.

"A pleasure meeting you, Doctor," he said.

"Likewise. Comin', Jessica?"

"Yes. Good-bye Detective Calid. And thank you for everything you've done."

"Give a call before you head home," he said.

"I'll do that," I said.

A taxi dropped us in front of my villa at Lover's Lagoon Inn. "Hungry?" Seth asked.

"No. You?"

"Famished."

"Then why don't you go next door and have something to eat. Don't overdo it," I added. "We'll have dinner together tonight."

"At Diamond Reef?"

"Any place but." I fished my St. Thomas guidebook from my bag and handed it to him. "Pick a good restaurant, and make a reservation for seven. Okay?"

"Ayah. I'll do that. What are you about to do?"

"Relax, think a little. And there's someone I really need to talk to."

Chapter 24

Laurie Marschalk was in the inn's kitchen when I sought her out. I quietly stood in the doorway and watched as she carefully cut thin strips of meat with a large carving knife, tossing them in with other ingredients already in a large, round stainless-steel bowl. So engrossed was she in her task that she was oblivious to my presence.

"Laurie," I said.

She stopped cutting but didn't turn, just stood like a statue, the knife's motion frozen in midair.

I stepped into the kitchen. "Whipping up something special?" I asked.

She allowed the knife to fall onto the table, faced me, wiped her hands on her Lover's Lagoon Inn apron, and said, "I thought you were going home."

"Oh, I am. Perhaps tomorrow. But before I do, there's something we should talk about."

"No there isn't."

"I saw you at the dock at Pettyklip Point today," I said.

My statement impacted her. Her eyes opened wider, and her mouth became a severe slash across her pretty face.

"I saw you there with Mr. Webb, Senator Jensen, and Mark Dobson from Diamond Reef."

"So what? I can't believe this, Jess. What are you, hell-bent on destroying me? I've lost my husband to a crazed murderer. Isn't that enough?" I started to answer but she raised her voice and demanded, "What is it you want from me?"

"The truth."

"The truth about what?"

"About Walter's murder. You knew all along it was Fred Capehart who'd killed him."

Her forced laugh was ineffective.

"You know, Laurie. Why you didn't turn him in is one thing. But more important is why you allowed that innocent young man, Jacob Austin, to be accused and jailed for a murder he didn't commit?"

She said nothing.

"Did you know that Capehart and Mark Dobson intended to kill Jacob this afternoon, discard him into the sea?"

"No, I didn't," she said in almost a whisper. "Is he—?"

"Dead? No. Seth and I rescued him."

It was as if someone had suddenly pulled a plug from an air-filled pool float. All the air came out of her, and she sagged against the stainless-steel table.

I stepped closer, said, "No matter what you've done, Laurie, no matter what trouble it might bring, I am your friend. I didn't set out to make such accusations. I came to St. Thomas because dear friends had invited me. I came here to rest, laugh, share good moments with those friends. But life happens, as someone once said, while you're making other plans."

"It isn't like it seems, Jess."

"I'm sure it isn't," I said. "I know you had nothing to do with Walter's murder, or with the plans to throw Jacob Austin off the boat today. But why did Fred Capehart kill Walter? Because of the money owed him for having ghostwritten his books?"

"He didn't intend to—" She stiffened. "I don't have to explain anything to you, Jess. It happened. It's over. Life goes on. Life *must* go on."

"And life must not be taken. At least not by us here on earth."

A door at the other end of the kitchen opened, and Chris Webb and Bobby Jensen came through it. "Laurie, we just heard that—" They saw me and stopped.

"Jess is just leaving," Laurie said.

I faced the men. "What did you hear?" I asked. "That Jacob Austin didn't die at sea?"

"What have you been telling her, Laurie?" Jensen asked in more of a snarl than a voice.

"Nothing."

"The boat went down," Webb said.

"The boat? Went down?" Laurie said.

"No survivors. The Coast Guard just reported it."

"The boat with Jennifer on it?" I asked.

"And Fred—and Mark." Laurie reached behind her and picked up the carving knife she'd been using when I arrived. I involuntarily stiffened as she held it out in front of her, the blade pointed at me. Then, holding it in both hands, she raised it above her head. I didn't know whether she intended to lunge at me, or to drive the knife into her own chest. No one said anything. We were transfixed, three people waiting to see what would happen next.

"I'm so sorry, Jess," she said. Her body began to convulse as the sobbing commenced. The knife fell noisily to the tile floor as Laurie Marschalk, my friend for so many years, slowly sunk to her knees where she remained, body heaving, primordial sounds coming from her lips.

I knelt down and wrapped my arms around her. Webb and Jensen stood over us. "She'll be all right," I said. "Why don't you just leave us alone."

Chapter 25

"Hope you like this place, Jessica," Seth said after we'd been seated at Fiddle Leaf, a striking restaurant decorated in the colors of sea and sky, and situated on a canopied pavilion overlooking Charlotte Amalie.

The norte had passed, leaving behind a star-studded black heaven that created its own sparkling canopy.

"It's lovely," I said.

"I would have opted for a good steak house, but didn't find one to my likin' in the book."

"Just as well," I said. "You eat too much red meat as it is."

"Nonsense. One 'a these days they'll be sellin'—"

"Cholesterol pills," we said in unison.

I'd told Seth little of the hour I'd spent with Laurie Marschalk after Webb and Jensen had left. We'd sat in the living room of her home within Lover's Lagoon Inn, drank tea—and talked.

"So, what'd she have to say for herself?" Seth asked as our Caesar salads were served. According to the guidebook, the Fiddle Leaf was known for its Caesar salads.

"A lot," I replied, breaking off a piece of crunchy French bread. "She's devastated by what's happened. And she knows she's facing legal trouble."

"For what?"

"For withholding evidence, for one thing. For

conspiracy, for another. Obstruction of justice. At least murder won't be one of the charges. She had no idea about the plan to throw Jacob overboard. She'd been told exactly what Jacob had been told—that he was to be moved to the States, given money, and that his family would join him."

"Sounds like she got herself caught up with a den 'a thieves," he said, tasting his salad. "Real good," he proclaimed.

"I think that's an accurate assessment," I said, savoring a crouton from the salad and smacking my lips. "But you can't let Laurie off the hook that easy. She's been as ambitious and greedy as the rest. They were all consumed by greed. Capehart, Jennifer, Webb, and Senator Jensen. I spoke with Adrian Woodhouse at the newspaper. He says he's going to call for a new investigation into the whole sordid mess, including the three-year-old murder of that old man, Caleb Meseau."

"From what I saw at Laurie's dinner party, Mr. Woodhouse was in pretty tight with the rest 'a them."

"I asked him about that. He claims he pretended to be friendly with Laurie and the others in order to get close and find out more. Whether that's true or not is conjecture. I just hope he follows through and exposes all the shenanigans that have gone on, including Jensen's involvement."

"I second that."

"He'll have plenty to write about. Do you know what Laurie told me, Seth?"

"I'm listenin'."

"This deal with Diamond Reef is a lot bigger

than simply having the inn taken over by the resort. It's a true merger, with big stakes. Laurie will end up part owner of Diamond Reef, along with Webb and Jensen. That's what's really behind everything that's happened."

"Go on."

"Jennifer—poor thing—came here to confront Walter about the money he owed her for helping write his travel books. Capehart originally declined to come with her, but changed his mind. He held the key to everything. Even Jennifer didn't know that Walter had signed an agreement with Capehart giving him a percentage of any resort Walter opened. Of course, that was before Lover's Lagoon Inn became a reality.

"Capehart decided to pull out his trump card. He rung Jennifer in, and she agreed to be with him when he laid that card on the table for Walter.

"They met with Walter that night at the lagoon. Things got nasty. Unfortunately, Capehart had found a straight razor that afternoon on the grounds, the one Jacob had bought as a gift for his grandfather, and then lost. Things got out of hand, and Capehart lashed out with the razor. That was it for Walter."

"How do you know all this, Jess?"

"From my conversation with Laurie. Jennifer, who was there when it happened, was horrified. She didn't know what to do, so she turned to Laurie and confided in her. Told her every intimate detail of what had happened, and the background that led to it. It must have been difficult for Laurie to throw in with Jennifer. After all, Jennifer had been one of Walter's many mistresses. But when money this big is involved, those other niceties go by the wayside."

Our waitress took our order for main courses—a rack of lamb for Seth, Caribbean lobster for me despite Seth's suggestion that I wait until getting back to Maine before having lobster.

"Let me see if I understand this," Seth said. "Capehart was an unwelcome partner in the inn by virtue of the written agreement he had with Walter."

"Exactly. That was Walter's way of avoiding having to pay Capehart for the work he'd done on his books. Jennifer was in the same position of having been stiffed, as they say, only Walter hadn't promised her anything like he promised Capehart."

"So Capehart kills Walter, then plays that trump card you mentioned to get off the hook."

"Right again, Seth. He—and Jennifer—got Laurie to go along with Capehart's scheme to have the murder pinned on someone else, namely Jacob Austin, who was known to harbor dislike for Walter. Don't forget, Walter had fired Jacob that morning, and everyone knew it. *And,* Capehart had used Jacob's razor to kill Walter."

A trio of musicians began playing soft Caribbean music, adding to the restaurant's genteel, tranquil ambiance. "Are you up to a swing around the dance floor?" I asked.

"Will be, Jessica, soon as you answer a couple of more questions."

"Shoot."

"Walter's murder was blamed on Jacob Austin. He's in jail. This Doctor Silber turns out to be no help at all. Capehart and his colleagues even have the murder weapon, a razor belonging to Jacob."

"Yes?"

"So why decide to concoct a story that he killed himself, and then try to spirit him off the island?"

"Because they couldn't be sure he'd be convicted, Seth. Not only that—and I'll take some credit for this—my being here and—well, let's call it snooping, as Laurie has been saying— put a certain pressure on them. If Jacob was believed to be dead, the authorities would consider the Marschalk case closed. It really wasn't hard to put that plan into action. Senator Jensen had the clout, and the money to buy off Doctor Silber, first to 'forget' Jacob's call to him the night of the murder, and then as medical examiner to sign Jacob's death certificate. He also bought the guard, Butch, and anyone else necessary to make it work."

"Only they didn't figure on havin' Jessica Fletcher on the case," Seth said.

I laughed. "I wasn't 'on the case,' as you put it. I just happened to come to St. Thomas on a vacation. They had a case of bad timing."

We enjoyed our entrées, and topped off dinner with heavenly chocolate soufflés.

"Ready for that spin on the dance floor?" Seth asked, standing and holding out my chair.

"Well, my dance card is pretty full, but I think I can squeeze in one more. After all, I am on vacation."

IF YOU HAVE ENJOYED READING THIS
LARGE PRINT BOOK AND YOU
WOULD LIKE MORE INFORMATION
ON HOW TO ORDER A WHEELER
LARGE PRINT BOOK, PLEASE WRITE
TO:

WHEELER PUBLISHING, INC.
P.O. BOX 531
ACCORD, MA 02018-0531